Skateboard Blues

Sydell Lowell Voeller

Published by Sydell Voeller, 2024.

This is a work of fiction. Similarities to real people, places, or events are entirely coincidental.

SKATEBOARD BLUES

First edition. March 1, 2024.

Copyright © 2024 Sydell Lowell Voeller.

ISBN: 979-8224259809

Written by Sydell Lowell Voeller.

Dedicated to the skateboarders of the mid-1970s through the 1980s when skateboard parks first made their debut.

Chapter One

"Jessica, stop being so snoopy!"

I jerked back from my bedroom window, gritting my teeth. Sometimes I felt like telling my pesky ten-year-old sister that she was the snoopy one. Couldn't I do as I pleased without Angie always poking her nose into my room?

"Be quiet, Angie. Who says I can't look out my window?" I gave my shoulder-length light brown hair a shake and pulled back the curtain a little farther.

My gaze riveted on the new family across the street. A big yellow moving van was parked in front of their slate-colored Victorian house, commonly known as the old Schrader place. Several people were dashing in and out, carrying crates and cardboard boxes. Behind the van, someone had parked a white Mercedes with a California license plate. Next to it stood a midnight blue Porsche.

"Snoopy, snoopy, snoopy. That's what you are," Angie persisted in her high-pitched voice. "What if they see you spying on them?"

"So what?" I couldn't help thinking she was more annoying than the buzzing, half-dead fly caught between my window and the screen. I picked up the fly inside a wad of Kleenex, opened the screen, and shook it outside. Wouldn't it be great if you could get rid of little sisters just as easily? I figured it was worth a try. "Hey, Angie, Mom's calling."

She stuck out her tongue. "Don't lie to me! Mom's still at the library. She's working later than usual today."

I flashed her an evil glare, hoping she'd get the message and take off. Just because she got straight A's and was the smartest kid in Mr. Alexander's fifth grade class didn't excuse her from being a smart aleck. I could run my life without her expert advice.

No luck. Angie carelessly brushed my side, then plopped down on my yellow quilted bedspread, crossed her legs, and stared at the ceiling.

I did my best to ignore her. Looking again across the street, I shaded my eyes against the October sun. Dust motes danced in the shaft of light streaming through my window.

A guy with sandy blond hair appeared from the neighbor's garage. Toting a skateboard under one arm, he wore black sweats and a red T-shirt emblazoned with a jumble of brightly-colored designs.

The guy strode to the driveway. With a toss of his head, he hopped onto the skateboard. Wheels clacked against pavement as he roared down the incline, zigzagged up the neighboring driveway, then twisted and shot back down onto the sidewalk. There he jumped over two cardboard boxes and landed in perfect control. I couldn't take my eyes off him. He was gorgeous—and practically a pro skater!

Angie started chanting a dumb song about a bear in tennis shoes she'd learned at camp last summer. I knew she was doing it to irritate me, but I refused to let it. I was determined to keep watching that gorgeous guy across the street.

Board-in-hand, he emerged from the shadows of a maple tree. I squinted, trying to make out the designs on his shirt. Something about skateboarding, no doubt.

What I wouldn't give for him to look up here and notice me. Or better yet, meet me face-to-face. Yet the idea of that really happening filled me with panic. What would I say? What would I do?

Suddenly the thought of facing him seemed more nerve-wracking than the day last year in school when I had to speak in front of the entire student body. I was running for freshman class secretary and almost threw up in the girls' locker room while I was waiting for my turn. After an experience like that, I couldn't understand why my father, a dentist, had decided to run for mayor of Preston. My attention shifted back to the boy with the skateboard, and I got a strange quivery feeling inside. I knew it was time to get my act together. Leaving Angie singing louder than ever, I raced downstairs, headed for the utility room, and grabbed a bucket and sponge out of the closet. It was a golden fall afternoon—perfect for washing the car!

My hands tingled from the icy water that blasted from the hose, and the wet driveway felt rough beneath my bare feet. Sunshine warmed my back.

As I was soaping down the hood of the car, I kept looking across the street. A man dressed in blue and white pin-striped coveralls poked his head out of the van and called to the boy with the skateboard. The guy dropped the board, climbed up into the truck, and started helping the man tug an oversized couch off the back.

It didn't appear as if things were going too well. The sheet, partially draped over the couch, kept getting caught underneath it. They had to stop every few minutes to yank the sheet free.

I guessed they must be father and son. The man called the skater Cam.

To me, the typical guys at school had become boring. They were all wrapped up in their backward ways or stuck on acting preppy. There'd never be anyone in Preston worth dating, I'd told myself. I couldn't help wondering if they'd included a job description for nuns in my careers survey class. *But now?* I glanced again across the street, and my stomach fluttered. Now maybe things would be different.

As I yanked at the hose, I watched Cam out of the corner of my eye. In between snatches of conversation with his dad, he looked over at me and grinned. My pulse raced.

The pounding of skateboards, mingled with the clattering of wheels, drew nearer. Three more skaters whizzed into the driveway at the old Schrader house. *This guy works fast*, I thought. Already he's made new friends! Maybe there was hope for me.

"Jessie!" I'd been so busy watching the new neighbors, I hadn't even heard my sister approach from behind me. "Megan's on the phone."

"Okay! I'll be right in." I flicked soap suds off my hands and dashed inside the house.

"Hey! What's going on?" Megan asked after I'd answered the phone.

"I'm washing the car and watching the new neighbors move in." I wasn't sure whether I was ready to tell her about the cool guy yet. Megan had flowing blonde hair that looked like corn silk, and her figure was terrific. All she had to do was flash her round blue eyes a time or two, and any guy she wanted would be beating down her front door. The last thing I needed was competition.

"Want to go with Mom and me to the mall tomorrow?" she asked. "The stores are celebrating Super Sale Sunday. I'm planning to look for a sweater to go with my new jeans."

"Sounds terrific!" I ran a hand through my hair, stalling for time. If only there was some way I could get out of helping my family distribute campaign flyers, but I knew there wasn't. Dad said he depended on me. "However, I'm afraid I can't go with you," I added. "There are only a little over two weeks left to get out my father's campaign stuff."

"Again? You're always helping with the campaign." She let out an audible sigh. "I'll be glad when the election's over."

"Me too. *Especially* me. Consider yourself lucky you don't have a father in politics."

"I do, I do." She paused. "What are your new neighbors like?"

"Ummm . . . well, interesting."

"Interesting! Is that all you have to say? Interesting?"

Giggling into the phone, I answered, "Yeah, that's all I'm saying for now." I liked to keep Megan in suspense.

We talked a while about the weird new teacher in sophomore English who'd taken over for Mrs. Craxton after she'd left to have her baby and what a big zero the homecoming dance had turned out to be. But what could you expect from a backwards little school like ours?

Gravel crunched outside. I glanced through the front room window and saw Mom turn our van sharply into the driveway. I gulped, realizing I'd left the bucket, sponge, and a pile of polishing rags directly in her path.

I told Megan good-bye and bounded down our porch stairs. In the driveway my mother had already stopped the van, a perturbed look crossing her face.

"Hold on! I got it!" I scooped up the bucket. By now the sun had dried the soap suds onto the car's black paint job, and I knew I'd have to start all over. Oh, well! At least it gave me an excuse to still be out in the front yard.

I peered over at the slate-colored house again, but everyone had gone inside. So far, my plan to get Cam to see me wasn't working too well. I'd have to think of something better.

That night after I'd stuck the last utensil into the dishwasher, it dawned on me. Why not get started passing out Dad's flyers right away? Who said we'd have to wait? Besides, Mom and Dad had made plans to take Angie to a movie, so I'd finally be on my own. I was certain I could cover at least six square blocks before it got too late, and of course, my main target would be Cam's place!

I shared my plan with my mother as she folded sheets in the laundry room. Of course, I didn't say anything about my real intentions. Mom would never understand.

"Good idea, Jessie." Mom beamed at me as if she couldn't believe my sudden enthusiasm, then went back to stacking the laundry. "The earlier we get started the better," she added.

"Right. Projects like this take organization. I'll start tonight by covering the streets between our house and the highway."

She looked appropriately impressed. At first I thought she might object to my being out alone at night, but she didn't. In a small town like ours, everyone knows everyone, so I guess that's what she was thinking too.

"I see the new neighbors moved in today," Mom commented matter-of-factly. "I should take over one of my pineapple upside down cakes." She shook out a towel and closed the clothes dryer door with a thud.

"Hmmm. Guess so." I tried to sound noncommittal, but the clatter of skateboards drifting in through the opened window caused my voice to squeak. I wasn't in the mood for anymore lectures about the evils of skateboarding. Mom and Dad were really into keeping our town the quiet, dull place it'd always been, and as a lot of the people in Preston saw it, skaters were nothing but big trouble.

I think the biggest civic event last year was when the census takers got to change the four-digit population figure to a five-digit one. Luckily, we lived only forty miles west of a real city, Portland. As far as I was concerned, it was forty miles too-far-away.

My mother's voice rose. "I understand city council officially banned skateboarding downtown."

Inwardly I groaned. Maybe the sound of the skaters had gotten her started.

"Too bad the city can't build a skate park somewhere," I said. "At least it'd give the kids a place to go."

Mom shook her head. "We don't need skateboarders anywhere in Preston."

"Oh, Mom." I sighed. "It really isn't *that* bad!" I remembered seeing at school a sticker slapped across one of the skater's notebooks: *Skateboarding is not a Crime.*

"I might not have thought so at one time," she said with a new edge in her voice. "But ever since poor old Mrs. Winthry was knocked down and injured by a skateboarder in front of Phillips Department Store, I've changed my mind. I'm glad this town is finally beginning to take a stand. We can't allow such carelessness to continue. And mark my words, if your dad is elected to office, he'll see the new law's enforced."

"It could've been an accident," I reminded her. I refused to believe that any skater would try to hurt a senior citizen on purpose.

"Well, what about those skaters who've been darting out in front of cars?" she continued. "I'm sure that wasn't an accident! Skateboarders have no business cluttering our town. They're nothing but a liability."

As she ranted on, anger rose inside me. Somehow it didn't seem fair. Take Cam, for instance. He impressed me as being a nice guy. I hated it when my parents made judgments.

Mom changed the subject and relief swept over me—but not for long. "I hope you don't mind taking Angie out with you tonight," she said.

"Angie!" I shrieked."Why do I have to drag *her* along? I thought you were taking her to a movie."

"Plans have changed. Ellie McFarlan invited Angie over tomorrow afternoon for a birthday party, and they're going to see the show then. In the meantime, Dad and I promised the Murrays we'd come over to play bridge."

"Oh, all right. I'll take Angie with me." I shrugged. Why did my little sister always have to mess up my life?

I gazed down at the stack of boxes Mom had brought home from the printers. Dad must have been planning to pass out flyers to our town's entire five-digit population, whether they were voting age or not!

I was tempted to stamp a few of the flyers with my favorite butterfly stamp, the one I used whenever I signed my name. Though I knew Dad would kill me if I did, the idea became increasingly appealing. To me, butterflies symbolized freedom and adventure. Someday—the sooner, the better—I'd break free of my Preston cocoon. I'd lift my wings to the beckoning sun and explore the exciting new worlds that were now beyond my reach.

Hurriedly I retrieved my stamp and rose-colored ink pad from my room, stamped the top two flyers and then stuffed a bunch more into my book bag. I tried to think optimistically about the task ahead. Maybe it would go faster than I expected.

Soon my sister and I were trudging out the door, our practiced smiles plastered to our faces. A crescent moon inched higher into the sky, and the smell of the recently harvested hay in the field across the highway wafted our way.

"Where're we going first?" Angie wanted to know, charging ahead of me.

"We'll start with the houses on our side of the street," I told her. I figured it'd be a good way to ease into things. At least the two families next door knew us the best, and if I said something stupid, it wouldn't matter much.

"Can I talk to the people? Ple-a-s-e, Jessie!" Angie dropped a flyer, then ducked down to retrieve it.

"Wait till you hear me do it a few times." I marveled at the patience oozing from my voice. Already Cam's presence in the neighborhood was doing strange things to me. "Now don't forget to smile and look the people directly in the eye," I went on. "The worst thing we can do for Dad's campaign is to act lame."

To my relief, the first several stops went well. Even crabby old Mr. Weinstein took one of the flyers and managed to squeeze out a hint of a smile.

As we moved from one house to the next, I noticed the warm glow of lights and families moving about inside. I had to admit during a fleeting moment like that, Preston didn't seem so bad.

The sight of a brick house with a campaign poster staked on the front lawn stopped me in my tracks. Harry Kappleton for Mayor, it read. I hesitated.

"What's the matter?" Angie piped up.

"Those people are voting for Dad's opponent," I explained. "Maybe we should just skip—"

"No!" Angie protested before I could even get the words out. "We're going to all the houses." I had to admit, for once my sister had a point. Squaring my shoulders, I led the way past a well-trimmed hedge up to the front door. Moths flittered about the dim porch light.

I let Angie ring the door bell, but no one answered. She rang again. Then we heard heavy footsteps on the other side of the door, and a man with tousled hair and a wrinkled plaid shirt answered. I recognized him immediately. Harry Crosham from the Village Hardware.

"What do you want?" he demanded crossly.

Angie shrank back a little, but I held my ground.

"Uh . . . er . . . good evening, Mr. Crosham." Haltingly I began my usual spiel, but all the time I was thinking about not sounding lame. Unfortunately now, my advice wasn't doing any good.

Mr. Crosham soon cut me off. "Didn't you read the sign out front? Kappleton's getting my vote. Now scram, you two! Can't an old man ever have any peace and quiet these days?"

Hurriedly we turned back onto the sidewalk.

"I didn't like that man," Angie said under her breath.

"Me either." Then a horrible thought struck me. What if Cam's family was equally rude? What if his mom or dad told us to take off too? It was enough to make me want to change my mind about going over there.

In minutes the old Schrader place loomed before us. A chill coursed down my back. Was it from the brisk autumn air or was I really going to chicken out?

The moving van was no longer parked in the driveway, and the front yard appeared empty compared to the frenzied activity a few hours earlier. Even the Mercedes and the Porsche were gone. Near the side of the house, not far from the hedge, I thought I saw something move, but it was too dark to be sure.

"That's the new neighbors you said were spying on!" Angie pointed at the house.

"Shh!" I clapped my hand over her mouth. "Watch it, will you? You know perfectly well I wasn't spying. We've been over that already."

"Why should I shut up?" Angie whined.

"I never told you to shut up. I said—"

"Hey! Selling Girl Scout cookies or something?" A guy's voice sounded from behind us.

It had to be Cam.

Chapter Two

I turned around and stared into Cam's face. The porch light made his greenish eyes sparkle. "Of course not." My voice rose. "I quit Girl Scouts *ages* ago!" Not only was I making a complete fool of myself, I was also forgetting the speech I'd been silently rehearsing.

"Sorry if I startled you," he said. "I was in the backyard trying to see if there'd be room to build a half-pipe. Then I discovered I'd locked myself out. I was just coming around to try the front door." He leaned his skateboard against a porch-type wicker chair. The skateboard's deck was red with designs of fire-breathing dragons.

"It didn't look like anyone was home," I explained. "We were about to leave."

"Well, I'm glad you didn't." He moved a little closer. "My name's Cam. We just moved in today."

"She already knows that!" Angie exclaimed. I had all I could do to keep from hitting her.

"Hi, Cam." I could feel my face growing hot, but by then I was finally starting to gather my senses. "I'm Jessica Williams. This is my little sis, Angie. We live in the house across the street."

"Jessica. I like that. Do they ever call you Jessie?"

"Uh, well sure. I mean, some of my friends do." I could feel Angie fidgeting next to me, and I prayed she wouldn't say something stupid again. Cam seemed interested in me.

He twisted the brass doorknob and shook his head. "Locked too. Oh, well! Guess I can camp on the front porch till my folks get home." He looked down at my flyers. "So if you're not selling cookies, then what do you want?"

"Angie and I are campaigning for my dad. He's running for mayor." I handed him a flyer.

He stuffed it into the pocket of his jeans. "Mayor, huh? Sure, I'll be happy to recommend him to my folks." His gaze met mine. "Have you lived in Preston long?"

"All my life. But I plan to get out first chance I can. I'm sick of this small town."

He broke into a grin. "I hope you're not telling that to everyone. It doesn't exactly sound cool if you really want your dad to win."

"I know, I know." Already I'd messed up. It was obvious I hadn't impressed him yet.

"Hey, maybe you need a little help with this campaign. I'm not exactly the student body president type, but at least we could talk and that might make the time go faster. Besides, I've got to find something to do till I can get back into the house."

"Great idea!" I bit my lip, hoping I hadn't appeared too eager. *You might not think this is so cool if you knew how my dad feels about skateboarders.*

"We don't need you to come along," my sister chimed in. "We're doing perfectly fine, thank you."

"Angie, don't be rude! Cam can help if he'd like to. Besides, he's locked out of the house," I added pointedly.

"Why can't he climb in through the bathroom window like you always do?" she shot back.

Disgusted, I darted her another look, but Cam only laughed. "I've already tried that. I'm afraid the bathroom window's locked too. But if you don't want me to come with you . . ."

"Oh, we *do*!" I said. "Besides, it'll give you a chance to check out your new neighborhood."

As we walked down the steps back onto the sidewalk, Cam tucked his skateboard under his arm. "I've already met some dudes who live a few blocks away," he said.

"The skaters who came to your house?"

His eyebrows shot up in surprise, but he said nothing.

"I saw them while I was outside washing the car today," I explained. My face grew hotter by the second, and I silently prayed he couldn't see me blushing. Somehow, this conversation wasn't going right.

"Yeah. You must mean Pete and Andy. On our way into town this morning while we stopped to gas up, I saw them skating behind the service station and went over to talk with them. I told them where I live." A pleased expression crossed his face. "Guess they didn't waste any time looking me up."

We started down the street, Angie trailing close behind.

"Where's your family?" I asked.

"Jessie, that's none of our business," Angie put in airily.

"My folks went out to pick up a pizza and a few groceries." He chuckled. "Mom says I won't be fit to live with till there's food in the house."

In the gathering dusk, the branches of the maple tree above us stirred and cast shadows onto the sidewalk. Thank goodness, we still had a few blocks to go until we came to the part of town Angie and I hadn't already canvassed. That would give Cam and me some time to talk before I had to get back to business.

"You're a cool skater," I told Cam. "I couldn't help noticing when I was outside this afternoon." Of course I didn't tell him I'd also been watching him from my bedroom window before that.

He pushed back a strand of hair from his forehead. "Thanks. Maybe you already know this, but there's a skateboard shop in Portland, New World Skates. I'm going to check it out and see if they can use some weekend help."

"You'd be perfect for a job like that," Angie said.

I struggled to hold back my growing exasperation with her. Although Angie's comments were innocent enough, I couldn't help feeling she was trying to come between Cam and me.

He stopped walking for a moment and winked at her. "Well! I'll even tell the boss you said so."

"It must've been terrible having to move," I said. "Especially to a small town like ours." Again, I didn't want to let on how a lot of people in Preston felt about skaters. "Where'd you come from?"

"California. Santa Cruz."

"That's near Disneyland!" Angie put in. "We went to Disneyland a long time ago, didn't we Jessie?"

I swatted her playfully. "You got that all wrong, silly! Santa Cruz is about three hundred miles from Disneyland."

I turned to Cam. "But my sister's right. Going to Disneyland has been our one-and-only trip outside of Oregon so far."

He smiled, showing the dimple in the cleft of his chin. He was even cuter than when I'd first seen him from a distance. We moved aside to let a couple of joggers pass by.

"Do you miss California?" I asked.

"Yeah, sometimes. We've moved a lot though. My dad's the type who likes to climb the corporate ladder. Gotta go where the opportunities are, he always says."

I thought about the white Mercedes and the dark blue Porsche. Obviously, Cam's dad hadn't missed a beat.

"So his current opportunity is in Preston?" I asked, confused as to how that could be.

"No, he got a job at a software company in Portland. But when we were looking for a place to live, my folks decided they liked Preston, especially since it's on the route to the coast."

I nodded. "It sounds like you've been all over." We stopped at a crosswalk and waited for a red sports car to roar by.

"Almost *all over*," he answered. "Some kids hate having to change schools so often, but I don't." For the next several minutes, he talked about his exciting past—skating the upper hills in Hawaii, doing freestyles for slalom races in Santa Cruz, snowboarding down mountain slopes in Colorado.

"You're so lucky," Angie said.

"I second that," I put in. My gaze swept our street of old homes fronted by tree-lined sidewalks. I couldn't help wondering if it looked dull to Cam after everything he'd known before.

"Why didn't you look at the campaign flyer?" my sister asked.

"Angie!" I shrieked. "Cam can read it whenever he wants to!"

He held up a hand and chuckled. "Hold on, you two!" He fished the flyer out of his pocket and read aloud the bold-faced print: "Arthur Williams, dentist, community leader, and father of two, pledges his unfaltering dedication to every man, woman, and child in the town of Preston." He broke off. "Hey, Jessie, why did your father stamp these flyers with a butterfly in the corner?"

I snickered. "Oh, he didn't."

"Well, *somebody* did!"

Angie giggled, but remained quiet.

"Yeah, it was me," I said. "But I only stamped a few. I never thought you'd get one of them."

"So what do butterflies have to do with his campaign?"

I hesitated, biting my lip. Could Cam really understand my hopes and dreams? Hopefully he wouldn't laugh like some of my friends did when I told him what that butterfly symbol meant to me. Inhaling deeply, I proceeded with my story.

"I like your style," Cam said after I'd finished. "Most girls are too wrapped up in hairstyles and clothes to think about stuff like that."

A little thrill raced through me as I smiled up at him. "I like your style, too, Cam." For the next few minutes, we ambled along in comfortable silence. It was a wonderful feeling just knowing that Cam accepted me the way I was. I'd never thought I'd find a guy who did.

When we were safely out of my neighborhood where people weren't as likely to recognize me, I said, "I'm dying to see you skate again. Show us what you can do."

He flashed me a high voltage smile. "You mean that? You really want to see me skate?"

"Absolutely!"

"Yeah, Cam! Show us what you can do," Angie echoed.

"Okay then. Here goes!" He flipped his board onto the cement, sprinted after it, and leaped on, accelerating with a few hard kicks. Then he jumped high, spun in mid-air, and landed back on the pavement like a pro. The clacking of his wheels grew louder as he skated back to us.

"Wow!" I exclaimed. "I'd give anything to do that."

"Maybe someday you can. That is, if you're willing to work at it."

"Look, Cam! Watch this!" Angie started turning cartwheels on the lawn.

"Ignore her," I muttered to him under my breath. "It works every time."

He laughed. "I think your little sister's trying to upstage me. Maybe she's the one who should be learning how to skate!"

"Do *you* have a little sister?" I asked, hoping he'd understand.

"No, my folks decided one kid was enough." He flipped up one end of his skateboard, catching it in his hand. "Besides, we move around too much."

"But you don't mind moving," I pointed out. "Maybe if you'd had brothers and sisters, they wouldn't either."

He shrugged. "Possibly, but I doubt it. Most kids I know hate to move. I guess I'm different."

Silently I agreed. He was different all right—in more ways than he probably realized—and it was driving me crazy.

For the next hour or so, we walked from one block to the next passing out the flyers. As we came to each house, Cam stayed on the sidewalk while Angie and I talked to the people who answered the door. It was working out well. So far, no one had appeared to notice Cam's skateboard, so I felt relieved that I wasn't ruining Dad's campaign.

By then it was almost totally dark, so we decided we'd better head home. Crickets chirped from the overgrown grass in an empty lot.

Glittering stars studded the dark blue sky. As we wandered down the street, taking in the heavenly smells of someone's roses, Cam's hand brushed against mine. Too bad Angie was tagging behind us.

It was a perfect night for romance.

Chapter Three

"Jessie, wait up!" Megan's voice sounded above the after-school clamor in the hallway at Preston High.

I glanced over my shoulder. "Hurry! I don't have much time." I was making a bee-line for my locker before meeting Cam at his. Things were going better than ever. All week he'd met me before school by the courtyard fountain to walk me to first period. We often ate lunch together in the cafeteria too.

"You planning to run a marathon or something?" my friend asked. She was wearing her maroon shorts and matching T-shirt, the official dress for the girls' volleyball team.

"Maybe I am," I answered mysteriously. I glanced towards the end of the wing where Cam and his friends were talking and added, "the finishing line is at the end of the hall."

"What are you talking about?" She narrowed her gaze and frowned.

I figured it was time to break the news. Megan had been out of school most of the week with the flu, so she hadn't seen Cam and me walking around school together. For some odd reason, the news hadn't leaked out to her.

"See that guy with the blond hair, black jeans, and red high-tops standing at the end of the hall?"

"Sure. What about him?"

"That's my new neighbor!" Megan waited while I twirled my combination lock and yanked the locker door open.

"Not bad!" she breathed. "Have you met him yet?"

"Uh-huh. Last Saturday while I was passing out campaign brochures for Dad." I went on to explain about our meetings at the fountain and how terrific I felt when I was with him.

"No wonder you didn't want to go to the mall," Megan said. "You had it planned all along, didn't you? About meeting him, I mean."

"Mmmm, how'd you guess?" I dug through the clutter on the locker floor and pulled out my green vinyl-covered notebook, the one with my favorite butterfly design.

"What's his name?"

"Cam. Cam Easton." He and his family moved up from California.

"I think I've seen him around," she said. "He's got the same lunch period as I do. But that's not all. Last week after school one day, I noticed Mr. Crosham, that guy from the hardware store, chasing him and his buddies out of the parking lot. They were trying to skateboard there."

"Doesn't surprise me. The skaters don't stand a chance in this town." I sighed. "But I think Cam's gonna turn things around here."

"How so?"

"He's almost a pro skater. There's something about him. Something sort of worldly, you know? Maybe it's because he's moved around, lived in lots of different places."

"So has Joel Ramsey. He's an army brat."

"Yeah, but Joel's not with it like Cam is. Cam knows what he wants in life and where he's going."

She pushed a lock of auburn hair behind her ear and quirked an eyebrow. "Out chasing butterflies again, huh Jessie?"

I hugged my notebook more tightly against my chest. I didn't want Megan to see the butterfly design on the cover nor my assignment papers with my butterfly-inscribed signature. Though I knew she'd seen them dozens of times before, I wasn't in the mood that day to be teased.

"Maybe you should look for some adventure in your life too," I said. "Especially if it means meeting someone exciting like Cam." Someday, fifty years later when my friends woke up and found themselves still stuck in the same old place, they'd be sorry.

"Okay, okay." Megan threw up her hands in defeat. "Sorry I mentioned it."

Streams of kids swept past us, and the noise level was becoming higher by the second.

I brushed off her words with a knowing smile. "Actually, besides Cam being the cutest, most exciting guy I've ever met, I've got a good reason for wanting to talk to him again."

"What?"

"I'm going to ask him to teach me to skate!"

"Jessie, are you crazy? Your folks will disown you for sure. You know how caught up in public images they are right now." She knew my parents nearly as well as I did. For them, my becoming a skater would be the death of Dad's campaign.

"I don't care. Cam's worth the risk. Besides, it's time this town woke up and recognized the skaters for what they really are!" I fumed. "They're not muggers, druggies, or punk gang members like everyone seems to think. They're simply a bunch of kids who love skating and want a safe place to do it."

I jerked my head back towards Cam's locker. He was gone! Leaving my friend with her mouth gaping, I spun on my heel and shot down the hallway to catch up with him.

* * *

"Ou-whee-ouch!" I yelped. I blinked hard, wondering why it never occurred to me that cement was so hard. Thank goodness, I'd landed smack dab on my bottom where I had a little cushioning. The thrashed-up skateboard Cam had loaned me lay upside down about three feet away, wheels spinning. Now that Saturday had arrived and there was no one around Preston High, Cam agreed to let me join him and his skating buddies there.

"Hold on, Jessie! I'm coming," Cam called. He'd been leaning against one of the pillars in the school courtyard, watching my progress.

I groped to stand up. Feeling like a klutz, I vowed out loud, "I'll learn to do it—even if it takes me a hundred years." I looked down at the palms of my hands. They smarted from where I'd caught myself on the pavement, and one of them was bleeding. I remembered thinking when I was a little girl that every time I skinned my knee, I was being punished for something bad I'd done. Though I'd long outgrown that idea, I reflected guiltily about my leaving the house with Cam that morning and telling my parents he was going to teach me to skate. They were nicer about it than I'd expected, but I knew beneath their even expressions, they wondered what had come over me.

Cam clasped my shoulders, his gaze meeting mine. "Are you okay?"

"Sure. But you never told me skating was like this," I grumbled, shivering against the autumn chill.

Shakily, I dusted off my jeans and shrugged. The blood was starting to trickle down my wrist.

"Let me look at your hand," he said.

"It's nothing that a little Bactine won't take care of." I tried to sound nonchalant.

He pulled out a wad of Kleenex from his back pocket and then took my hand in his. As he dabbed at my abrasion, I wanted to melt. So far, it was the closest we'd come to holding hands. Suddenly I no longer felt the pain.

His brows knit together in a frown. "Your first battle scar. Well, it looks clean. But you'd better soak it when you get home."

"Good thing your board's already thrashed up," I apologized. I picked up the chipped, well-used skateboard, examining it for new damage.

"No sweat," he said, grinning. "That board's seen a lot worse crashes than the one you just took." He gave my hand a quick squeeze. "Know something, Jessie?"

"Umm, what?"

"I think I like you." A thrill coursed through me. Though it seemed Cam and I had come from two opposite planets, I sensed we had a lot in common. My feelings for him were growing stronger by the minute.

He kept holding my hand even after Pete and Andy and the rest of the skaters crowded around us. It was worth it having fallen and crashed.

Pete punched me playfully in the ribs. "Hey, Jessica. Slow down! You trying to burn up the pavement or something?"

"Go easy on her, dude," Cam said. I thought I'd detected a hint of jealousy in his voice. "At least she's trying."

I attempted to pull off a joke about my crash landing, but I was still feeling stupid about it. At least the guys in Cam's crowd accepted me.

As Cam turned back to me, a concerned expression shadowed his face. "You're sure you still want to do this?"

"Of course, I'm sure. I don't give up easily!"

The rest of the crowd skated off towards the tennis courts.

"If you're really serious about skating, then you'll need to work on your ollies a little more." He nodded back to the curb where I'd first messed up. "Try it again. Then grind the edge of the sidewalk and shred back down the parking lot." He smiled crookedly. "When you get better at it, we'll work on some 180s and 360s."

"Whoa, slow down!" I burst into giggles, despite my injuries. "Let's take first things first." At least I was beginning to learn the skaters' language. Cam had already told me that grinding and shredding meant skating fast and hard. I wasn't ready for that. Furthermore, I couldn't even begin to fathom doing aerials.

He tossed his board down on the pavement. "Here, watch me. That's the best way to learn."

While I adjusted my helmet back into place—Cam had insisted I wear one—he made a running start on his board and zigzagged up a stretch of the driveway. Rotating twice at the top, he swooped up a concrete rise near the courtyard fountain, landed upright, and zoomed down the pavement. As he passed the glinting picture windows of the auditorium, he shouted over his shoulder. "Here's where I check out my reflection! If my clothes don't look right, I call my valet." He grinned. "Just teasing."

"Cam!" I clapped my hand over my mouth and giggled. "You're too much!"

"All *right*!" Pete yelled from where he and the other skaters were watching. "That's rad, Easton!" They skated back towards us.

"That was awesome, man!" Andy agreed.

"Let's go somewhere else," a guy by the name of Nick said. "We've skated this lot so many times, it's boring."

"Like where?" Cam asked, grinding to a halt. Sweat beaded his forehead.

Pete snapped his chewing gum. "How about the back of the old warehouse on Maple Street? Those loading ramps are perfect."

"Nah, we'll get kicked out of there in a minute," another guy answered.

Though I liked the skaters, I secretly wished they'd find somewhere else to go and leave Cam and me behind. I loved every moment we'd been alone, which hadn't been much so far. Yet I didn't dare tell him how I felt. What if he thought I was trying to own him, got cold feet, and took off?

"If only city council hadn't banned skating downtown," Andy said. "Ever since that kid—whoever he was—knocked over Claudia Morton's grandmother, we've been doomed."

Cam frowned in concentration. "I heard he was a dude from the junior high, right?"

"You got it," Pete answered. "But I doubt if it was as bad as everyone made it out to be."

I could tell already that Cam knew what the people of Preston thought about skaters.

"Maybe not," he said. "But it's up to us to make a difference. Sure, it's true skaters are sometimes radical. We've got our own music, our own clothes, our own way of talking. But the bottom line is: skateboarding is a challenge. It means testing the limits, being the best you can be. That's important stuff."

Andy made a face. "Get serious, Easton. You planning on running for student body president or something? Or maybe now that there's a girl hanging with us, you're pulling off the Mr. Impressive act."

A ripple of laughter rose up from the skaters.

"Hey, I *am* serious." Cam refused to be put off. "It's up to us to show the younger kids it's cool to be safe, it's cool to be polite and to stop when you see a senior citizen."

Andy snorted. "A lot of good that does us now. City Hall's already got their minds made up."

I was becoming increasingly uncomfortable. Any minute now, I was sure, someone would point out that my dad was running for mayor. Somehow, I felt totally out-of-place.

A shout of anger sliced through my thoughts. I looked over to the entrance of the school, just beyond the fountain. Our school principal, head lowered like a bull charging a matador's red cape, was marching directly towards us.

Chapter Four

During the following couple of weeks, our problems got worse. Everywhere our little band of skaters went, we were told to leave. It didn't matter whether it was the steep rise of blacktop on the south side of town, the empty city swimming pool that had been closed for lack of funding, or the parking lot behind the mortuary. All the shop owners were afraid we'd either knock someone down again or end up hurting ourselves.

Then, of course, there were my parents. Sometimes they let me skate with Cam, sometimes they didn't. I guess it just depended on what kind of mood they were in.

At least there was one bright spot. My crash landings were happening farther apart, so I knew I was making progress. Still, I couldn't help wondering where I stood with Cam. Though we'd been seeing each other almost every afternoon after school, most of our time was spent with the skaters. Was I, to him, just another neighbor kid on his block? Sure, he'd said he liked me, but maybe he told that to all the girls.

By the end of the week at school, my nagging doubts skyrocketed. It all started during my lunch period when Mike Thompson and Rocky Sherman, star football players, sauntered into the cafeteria and sat down across from Megan and me. I'd only talked to them a few times before because they were usually busy trying to impress the cheerleaders.

As I explained to Megan how I'd finally managed to master the mini-ramp we'd set up in Pete's driveway, I could feel them staring at me. They wore designer jeans and trendy cotton shirts and smiled their typical phony smiles. I supposed they expected us to pass out from throes of heart-stopping passion, but of course, we didn't.

"Hello, ladies," Rocky broke into our conversation. "May we have the honor of sitting with you?"

"Suit yourself," I answered with a shrug. The spicy smells of burritos wafted from the kitchen.

"So if it isn't Miss Skateboarder U.S.A.," Mike said, his gaze leveling on me. "Run over any little old ladies yet?" I ignored his question, plus the sarcasm dripping from his voice.

"And if it isn't the football heroes of Preston High," I replied coolly. "Every girl's dream." My flip response didn't appear to faze them.

"Tell me something, Jessica," Mike said, loading a mound of catsup onto his cheeseburger. "Is Cam Easton the one responsible for your new hobby?"

"New hobby!" I sputtered. "Listen here, Mike Thompson, skateboarding is more than a silly little hobby. A bunch more! You ought to try it sometime."

"Yeah, you ought to try it sometime," Rocky parroted in a falsetto voice, wiggling his eyebrows up and down. I wanted to hit him. Out of the corner of my eye, I could see Megan squirming.

"So answer the question," Rocky prodded. "Does Easton have anything to do with it or not?"

"Of course he does." I stared into Rocky's flashing dark eyes.

"Why are you even asking?" Megan jumped to my defense. "It's none of your business!"

Mike leaned a little closer, looking first at Megan, then at me. "Because girls like you shouldn't be so naïve. Don't you see what Easton's up to?"

I could feel my heart pumping faster by the minute. "What are you talking about?"

Rocky drawled. "It's as plain as the nose on your face. Cam's a skater, right?"

"Of course he is! So what?" I heaved a sigh. "I swear, you're like all—"

"Hold on. I'm not knocking skateboarders."

"Then what *are* you doing?"

"I'm simply trying to get you to wake up." He paused, and I sensed he wanted to make me squirm. "Cam's lived all over, right? He's skated almost every place on the continent."

"Don't forget Hawaii," Megan put in.

"I'm *so* impressed," he said with a sneer. "But the bottom line is this, ladies—good old Easton comes to town and discovers there's no place he can skate without getting kicked around." He lowered his voice dramatically. "Then he plays up to the mayor's daughter, makes her think she's really something, so eventually he can get on the good side of her old man—"

"Wait!" By then my face was flaming. "I get it now! But you're wrong. Dead wrong!"

"Wanna bet?" Mike chimed in. "Rocky's never wrong."

"Well, he is this time. For starters, my dad's not the mayor yet. And even if he were—"

"Oh, come off it, Williams," Rocky interrupted. "You know he's going to win. So why get hung up on a little technicality? The important thing is you can't afford to be so blind." Lunch trays rattled around us.

"Why don't you go pick on some silly little airhead cheerleader?" Megan stormed. "Leave Jessie alone."

My tuna and relish sandwich was sticking in my throat, and I felt as if someone had punched me in the stomach. "If you're saying that Cam's using me simply to get a skate park in Preston, you'd better think twice. He would never do a thing like that. He doesn't use people."

"Aw, love is so blind," said Rocky, holding his hand over his heart. He and Mike burst into laughter.

I stuffed my half-eaten sandwich back into my lunch sack. I couldn't take the humiliation any longer. Giving them an evil glare—the kind I usually reserved for only my sister—I jumped up from the table and flounced out the cafeteria door. In a flash, Megan had caught up to me.

"What's going on?" she asked as we almost ran head-first into our Phys-Ed teacher.

"It's simple." I turned down the corridor towards the rest rooms. "Cam's made a big impression at school. Lots of kids have watched him skate, and they know he's good."

"You mean they're jealous?"

"Exactly."

We scooted inside the john where I snapped on the spigot and splashed cold water over my flaming cheeks. "Next time those jerks give me any trouble, I'll really tell them!" I exclaimed. A senior who was putting on mascara darted me a curious glance.

"Maybe there won't be a next time," Megan said from inside one of the stalls. "You did a good job of putting them down."

"Thanks," I muttered. Yanking a paper towel out of the dispenser, I patted my face dry. My cheeks were still hot, my heart continued to pound. But worst of all, Mike and Rocky's words kept flashing little warning bells in the back of my mind.

* * *

Later that evening, as Cam and I walked hand-in-hand away from Pete's house, happiness washed over me. At last we were alone. I'd been waiting for this moment forever. Fleecy moon-lit clouds blanketed the purple sky, and the acrid smells of burning leaves drifted on the chilly night air.

We passed our town's small college, its ivy-covered, brick buildings nestled on a campus peppered with towering evergreens. On the opposite side of the campus, cheers burst forth from the grandstands where the football team was challenging its top rival. The stadium spotlights glared against the velvety darkness.

"My parents think I'm going to enroll at Markfield someday," I said, nodding towards the campus. "They're already talking about how I can live at home and save bundles on room and board."

Cam looked down at me, his eyes shining. "But that little butterfly inside you has different ideas, doesn't it?"

"Uh-huh. If I don't go to college at least a zillion miles away from here, then I'll travel and see the world." I met his gaze, hesitating. "What are you going to do after high school?"

He scratched the side of his nose, then grinned. "What is this? The Spanish Inquisition or something?"

I pretended to pout, though I knew he was only teasing. "Oh, Cam, don't be impossible. I just want to know you better."

"Okay. My plans for the future? Well, for starters, I hope to get sponsored and compete in the X games someday. That's my number one goal for now."

"You're talking about the action sports competition that's held in different places in the world, right?"

"Yep, that's it!"

"Cool! My family and I've watched the summer events on ESPN."

He nodded. "If I can become a pro, then I'll make enough money from skating to support myself. One thing I know for certain though. I don't want to climb the corporate ladder like my dad did. That's too boring—and too 'dog eat dog,' if you know what I mean."

"Maybe you'll start your own skateboard company someday too," I replied. "Then the only corporate ladder you'd have to climb would be your own."

He laughed. "Good point." Hunching his shoulders against the wind, he added, "Heck, maybe I'll build skate parks in African villages someday!"

"Oh, Cam, you're too much. Seriously, though, you're a born leader. I like what you said about watching out for senior citizens and setting a good example for the younger skaters." I wondered whether he agreed that we had a lot in common. To me, it was growing more apparent all the time we both craved adventure and new places.

We rounded the corner and wandered down our street. I wasn't in any hurry. I knew our house would be packed with my parents' friends who'd volunteered to help with the campaign.

In some ways, I was glad for that because it took some of the pressure off Angie and me. Now that we were getting down to the wire as far as the Big Day was concerned, the next strategy was phone canvassing. My parents had called a special meeting to get it organized.

Two kids on bikes whipped past us, and I lunged to the right to avoid a near collision.

"Woa!" I exclaimed. "And they accuse skaters of being reckless. Why isn't everyone up-tight about the bicyclists the way they are about skaters?"

"I hear you."

We strode past a sign that said, *No skateboards or bicycles on sidewalks.* Cam held my hand a little tighter. "Know something? We've got to figure out a way to get a skate park in Preston."

"Right, but how?"

"I'm not sure yet, but there's gotta be a way. When my family moved to California, the skate parks there were already built. But things are so much different in Preston."

"Maybe it wouldn't have to be a skate park," I said. "Maybe if we could just find a place where someone would let us build a half-pipe, then our problems would be over. It's great that we can use Pete's mini-ramp in his driveway, but that isn't enough. We need lots more room."

"Absolutely." He shifted his skateboard to the other side. "I'd like to build a half-pipe in my own backyard. But my dad says our place is too small. It's the same story for all the other skaters too. Either there just isn't enough room, or their parents aren't interested. I knew it'd be the laugh of the century to even think of asking my folks. Besides, Mom would never give up her rose garden that covered over half our backyard. Last year when Dad had wanted to build a swimming pool in its place, she'd nearly threatened divorce."

"I bet even if we could find a place to build it," I said, "the lumber would cost a bundle."

He nodded, but said nothing.

As we passed by the old homes on our street, I took in his sexy profile, his carefree gait. Daydreaming about what it'd be like to kiss him, I got this funny warm feeling inside. The only guy I'd ever kissed before was Jerry Butler, the boy I'd dated off and on last year. Like most of the other guys in Preston, he was totally boring. His kisses were that way too.

As we ambled up the steps to my house, the sounds of talking and laughter grew louder. Someone had left the front door open. Mom must've decided the house was getting too stuffy with all those people inside. At least no one had come out onto the porch for a breath of fresh air. Then, too, Angie was sleeping over at Priscilla McCumber's house, so I'd really lucked out. Maybe I could have Cam to myself a little longer.

"Can you stay for a while?" I asked Cam. "It's kind of crowded inside, so maybe we can just hang out here." I pointed at the green canvas lawn-swing where I sometimes sat on warm fall evenings, listening to the crickets chirping and just thinking things over.

"Sure. But maybe it'd be better if we went inside and offered to help."

My stomach dropped. "Uh . . . well, that wasn't exactly what I had in mind." I couldn't believe Cam wanted to get involved.

"Jessie, dear, is that you?" My mom's voice sounded from the dining room. "Who are you talking to?"

"Yes, I'm home!" I called back airily, but inside my hopes quickly faded. "Cam's here too."

Before I could add that we intended to stay out of everyone's way, Dad emerged with a big grin on his face. Looking more relaxed than

I'd seen him in ages, he wore his favorite fawn-colored sports coat. His salt-and-pepper hair was perfectly groomed.

"Hello, Cam." Dad shook his hand. "Nice to see you again. How're your folks adjusting to the new neighborhood?"

"Just fine, thank you. My mom, especially, really likes it here."

I looked away and rolled my eyes. Cam was talking about his mother, I reminded myself. Maybe she enjoyed a dull little town like ours after moving around so much.

"I hear you've been really busy with your campaign, sir," Cam continued.

"Ah, yes, but it's been worth every minute. My committee's terrific. Hard workers, every one of them." Dad rocked back on his heels and eyed Cam appraisingly. I could tell he was impressed. Maybe this would be a positive turning point for us.

"Tuesday's the day," you know, he added with a half-smile. "Be sure to remind your folks to get out and vote."

"Oh, I will!" Cam replied eagerly. "And about your campaign. Do you need any more help? Jessica and I'd be glad to pitch in."

A sinking sensation overcame me. Why was he still so eager? Unexpectedly the lunchroom scene at school flashed by me, and I fought back panic. Was my whole life flashing by me too?

Dad darted a look at our skateboards, raised his brow, then grinned. "That's great of you to offer, son. As a matter of face, we do have some loose ends to tie up. Why don't you kids come inside and join us right now?"

Before I could nudge Cam's side and send him a pleading look, Dad lowered his voice and added, "One request, please. Just leave your skateboards outside."

Chapter Five

"Don't answer it, Angie. I think that call's for me!" As I dashed to the phone in the kitchen, I caught my sister mumbling something and smiling into the receiver. I'd been waiting for Cam to call me all afternoon, but he hadn't.

"Sorry, Jessie can't talk to you now," she chirped. Now I could hear her all too well.

"Angie!" I sputtered, snatching the phone away from her. "I *can* talk to him! What's the matter with you?"

"Sisters!" I said to Cam. "Be glad you don't have any. I swear if Angie pulls this one more time, I'm outta here!"

He chuckled. "Maybe I should just come over instead of calling."

"Only if you can put up with our madhouse," I said. "I'll sure be glad when this election's over." At least things were looking up as far as Cam and my parents were concerned. In fact, he'd made a hit with the entire election committee.

As we talked, I glanced at his skateboard, the one he'd been letting me use. The yellow and red graphics that looked like zigzagging ribbons of fire were almost worn off. The edges of the deck were chipped and splintered.

"Cam?" I said.

"Hmm?"

"How much does a new skateboard cost? I'm afraid yours is going to fall apart any day now."

"Lots," he replied. "Especially if you want to buy a good board."

I gulped. I'd never be able to save up enough baby-sitting money.

"Speaking of new skateboards," he went on, "let's drive to Portland on Saturday. I'll show you the skate shop. The boss is supposed to be working then, and I'd like to check in with him too."

My heart leaped. At last a date—well, almost a date! "Oh, wow! I'd love it!" I cried.

"Okay, I'll pick you up at ten."

"Great! That'll give me—"

"Jessie, I need to use the phone," Angie cut in plaintively.

"You little rat!" I hissed.

Cam's laughter interrupted what could have been a knock-down, drag-out battle between my sister and me. At least *someone* was laughing.

"I'll call you back later," I told him with forced cheerfulness. I bolted down the hall and into her room.

"What's going on?" I demanded. I collapsed into the red vinyl beanbag chair next to her bookshelf. "Why don't you leave Cam and me alone? Don't you like him?" Maybe that was the problem. She liked him too much.

My sister was sitting cross-legged on her bed. Her lower lip protruded in a pout. "Sure, I like him."

"So what's the problem? Why are you always trying to mess up our time together?"

"Maybe it's because you're forgetting about me." Her voice rose. "*Everyone's* forgetting about me. All Mom and Dad talk about anymore is the election. And you're so busy with Cam, you're never around to take me to the movies or shopping for nail polish and earrings."

"Nail polish and earrings! Aren't you a little young for that stuff?"

She crossed her arms over her chest and lifted her chin. "Of course not! Mom promised me I can get my ears pierced when I'm eleven. That's only five-and-a-half months away. I'd like to get my earring collection started as soon as I can."

I smiled despite myself. Angie wanted to be grown-up so badly, but I couldn't blame her. I was like that when I was ten too. "Look, I'll make you a deal."

"What?" She pouted some more.

"If you promise to stay out of my business, I'll take you to Anderson's Deli and buy you an ice cream every Saturday. From now till Christmas."

"Nah. That's not so special. That's kid stuff."

"Then we'll go shopping for—"

She held up a hand and grinned. "Wait! I've got an even better idea!"

"What is it?"

"If you want to make me a deal, how about giving me some money?"

My stomach dropped. "But I need all the money I can get."

She appeared not to have heard me. "Every time Mom asks you to baby-sit me, you can give me part of what she pays you."

"I'll give you five dollars. That is if—I repeat, if—you keep up your end of the deal."

"Five dollars!" She sighed. "That's nothing. I bet if I were making a deal with Cam, he'd give me more than that."

I gritted my teeth. Obviously my sister was going to make this tough. "Okay, okay. I'll give you ten dollars. Right up until Christmas." Thank goodness that was only six weeks away. I'd endured lots worse for six weeks, I told myself.

"Yes!" she cried as she sprang off the bed. In seconds, she'd smothered me with hugs.

I felt relieved and frustrated all at the same time. Finally I'd won her cooperation, but the price was more than I'd expected. Now I'd never manage to buy a new skateboard. I could see my meager savings dwindling by the minute.

While the two of us consumed a big bowl of popcorn, we watched a movie on T.V. It was about a magical cat from outer space with blue shimmering eyes. The movie seemed to satisfy her, though she did keep reminding me it wasn't as good as the movie about a rock star she'd wanted to see at Priscilla's house and had to miss out. Because it was a school night, Dad had insisted she stay home.

After the movie, I tucked my sister into bed. "Sleep tight. Tomorrow's Dad's big day, you know."

"Night, Jessie," she said sweetly as I retreated from her room. "Thanks a bunch for everything."

"You're welcome."

I couldn't believe how angelic she sounded when things were going her way.

* * *

"We did it! We did it!" my mother cried, ending the phone call. "The last vote's been counted! Dad's the new mayor of Preston!"

Angie and I, who'd been sitting at the kitchen table doing homework, jumped up and cheered. Soon all four of us were laughing and hugging.

"Congratulations, Dad!" I kissed him on the cheek. "I knew you'd win. Even if Mr. Crosham wasn't voting for you," I added. I giggled, remembering the little fiasco on his doorstep the night Angie and I'd passed out flyers.

"Well," Dad said. He hitched his thumbs through his belt loops. "Now I can inform my office crew that we'll cut back to part-time hours. My receptionist will be overjoyed."

Mom hugged Dad one more time, her eyes shining with pride. "We're all thrilled for you, Ralph. You're going to be the very best mayor Preston ever had!"

Once the commotion had died down, Dad turned to me and said, "Sweetheart, there's something I've been meaning to ask you. A couple of nights ago, someone sprayed painted graffiti at the old empty Safeway. Do you know anything about it?"

"No, I don't," I answered, twisting a strand of hair around my index finger. I hadn't even seen it. The store stood on the east edge of town where I seldom went.

He pursed his lips. "The talk going around is that the skateboarders are responsible. Apparently, besides lots of vulgar language, the graffiti includes some skulls and crossbones."

My face flushed with anger. "But did anyone actually see who did it? It's not fair the skaters are always getting blamed!"

"The elderly woman who reported the incident never saw any skateboarders," Dad answered, "although she did witness about a half dozen youngsters fleeing from the scene. Are you sure you haven't heard any of Cam's crowd talking about it?"

"No! Absolutely not." I looked at him intently. "It's true that some of the skaters wear shirts decorated with skulls and crossbones, but it doesn't mean anything bad. It's simply part of the skater scene, one of the big manufacturer's trademarks. I don't know how the graffiti happened, but I'm positive none of Cam's crowd had anything to do with it."

His faced relaxed into a slow smile. "I believe you. Just keep your nose clean, okay, sweetheart?"

"Sure, Dad," I was quick to answer. But deep inside, resentment crept through me. Now I'd have to be the perfect child. Now I'd be living in my father's shadow.

All week long, our phone was always ringing or people were stopping by to congratulate Dad. Though I was happy for him, the constant fanfare got to me—especially the day the reporter from *The Preston Review* stopped by, a man by the name of Mr. Jack Thurston.

"Mr. Williams," the reporter said as he peered over his glasses. "As you know, recently there was a big problem at the vacated Safeway. Graffiti smeared from one end to the other. Reporters say the skateboarders in town are responsible. What's your opinion?"

Eavesdropping from the hallway, I held my breath. Dad had been right—people *were* blaming the skateboarders. Would he have the guts now to stand up for us?

"Well, Mr. Thurston," my father replied after clearing his throat. "As I'm sure you realize, the evidence is still inconclusive. Many of our skateboarders are responsible, law-abiding young people." He glanced at me and smiled. "I happen to know that for a fact. Let's not point any fingers just yet."

I wanted to cheer. I wanted to run into the front room and hug Dad right in front of that reporter and the important-looking photographer who'd arrived with him. I could just see it plastered on the front page of next week's paper: New Mayor, Ralph Williams, Supports Skateboarders.

* * *

"Jessica, dear," Mom said brightly, greeting me at the breakfast table Thursday morning. It was obvious she still hadn't come back down to earth. "Everyone is so thrilled about your dad becoming the mayor I just had to do something special."

"Like what?" I asked from behind the front page of our town's newspaper. I was reading an article about the graffiti at the old Safeway. Thank goodness, the reporter had refrained from blaming the skaters. Still, it seemed half the people in Preston were talking about us, insisting we were responsible.

"I've phoned Aunt Mildred and Uncle Ray in Seattle, Grandma and Grandpa Williams, and the entire election committee." She waved a long list about as she talked. "Everyone's coming here Saturday for a big celebration."

My stomach dropped. "Saturday?" It suddenly dawned on me I'd failed to tell my parents about my date with Cam.

"Yes, Saturday. I've ordered a huge turkey, a honey-basted ham, plenty of champagne, and called the caterer for the rest of the essentials. It's all set."

"Do I have to be at the party?" I asked. How could this be happening? After all my waiting and dreaming and even bribing Angie, how could one more thing get in the way?

My mother wrinkled her brow as she pushed a lock of auburn hair behind her ear. "Now what kind of question is that, Jessica Williams?"

"Hmm! I think I smell pancakes and sausage," a familiar voice cut into our conversation. It was Cam. Ever since I'd made my deal with Angie, he'd been stopping by each morning to drive me to school. My sister, who was determined to get every cent possible out of me by going along with it, had ushered him into the kitchen.

"Hey!" I greeted him, glancing at the clock on the wall. "You're kind of early, aren't you?"

"I thought maybe we could drive by the old Safeway before we go to school and check out the graffiti. After all, it'd be nice to see what we're getting blamed for," he added.

Apparently Mom was content to let his remark pass. "I was just telling Jessica about the celebration party we're planning on Saturday afternoon for Mr. Williams," she said to Cam. "Please consider yourself invited. Your parents too."

Frantically I met his gaze. How could we make her understand we had other plans?

"Couldn't we schedule Dad's party for Sunday instead?" I asked.

"No, that's out of the question. Your aunt and uncle have already made motel reservations for Saturday night, and Grandma and Grandpa are planning to come on the Friday afternoon train."

Cam sat down next to Mom. "The reason Jessica's concerned is because we planned to go to Portland on Saturday. For the whole day."

I relaxed, knowing I could count on him to pave the way.

"But we can always put it off for another time," he added. "I understand how hard you've worked—"

"Cam!" Just when I thought he was going to talk Mom into letting us go, he'd switched things around completely!

"She's right, Jessie." His voice rose with conviction. "This party's more important than our day in Portland. I can check in with the boss on Sunday instead." The dimple in his chin deepened as he smiled. "Besides, I want to be around when the election committee toasts your dad."

Chapter Six

We settled on a compromise. Cam and I'd stick around for the first hour of the party and then we'd be free to leave.

As I faced Saturday, mixed feelings churned inside of me. Though Dad had openly supported the skaters when he'd been interviewed by the reporter, I was certain everyone at the party would be talking about us. They'd say how terrible the graffiti at the old grocery store was, what rotten kids the skaters were, and how the ban on skating needed to be enforced further.

At the party, Cam and I raised our glasses of sparkling cider in a toast to my father and then retreated to a corner of the room to be with my grandparents, two of my favorite people. Grandma Williams was especially sympathetic when I'd told her about our plight. "Why, I've heard that in our neck of the woods, some of the high schools have sponsored skateboard teams," she'd said.

Wow! *Preston is still in the Dark Ages.* I gritted my teeth, but continued to smile.

By the time we were finally on our way, it was two-thirty. As we sped out of town in the Easton's Mercedes, I looked over at Cam and smiled. "So when will you know if you got the job?" I asked, thinking again about New World Skates.

"Maybe today." His emerald-colored T shirt made his eyes look even greener. "It'll be a great place to work. Just think, Jessie, I'll be right where all the action is. I'll be the first to know about the newest skateboards and all the local competitions."

"You certainly will." No doubt about it, Cam *was* an opportunist. But that still didn't mean he was using me, I reminded myself. "And one day the right person from a big skateboard manufacturer will be there and you'll be discovered," I went on. "Not only will they sponsor you on the spot, you'll get all the free boards you'll ever need for the rest of your life."

He chuckled. "You bet! What a deal!"

I looked out my side window as the wheat fields and orchards gave way to business parks and strip malls. Soon our conversation swung back to the graffiti. When we'd stopped by Thursday morning to look at it, Cam was as upset as I had been. It was a mess. Strings of profanity in black and purple and muddy brown spray paints stretched over half of the store's south side. We didn't see any skulls and crossbones, though, so we agreed that someone must've made that part up—just like all the other rumors about us.

"The graffiti happened at the worst possible time," he said as we sped through a tunnel that led to the city.

"Why?" I asked. "Is there any *good* time?"

"It's obvious. If we're going to try to wipe out people's preconceived ideas about skaters, this is going to make it tougher. I've been telling the others we need to be polite, we need to look out for the older folks, and then wham—someone decides to waste that old store." He frowned. "How can we expect to get a skate park when people think we're vandals?"

"Exactly. They'll just say we're destructive and irresponsible." I paused. "We might as well forget it. We don't stand a chance."

"No, Jessie." He pursed his lips. "I don't agree. If we don't fight for that skate park, then no one will. It's up to us."

Minutes later, after we'd followed the overhead signs into Portland, he parked the car in Old Town, one of the city's eclectic districts. Brick buildings lined the narrow sidewalks and weekend shoppers breezed past tattered old men who stood huddled together on street corners.

"Big cities are so interesting," I said as he took my hand in his and we started for the skate shop. "My family only comes here once in a while to see a concert or eat at Mom's favorite restaurant on the river." I hurried to match his long-legged stride.

"Dad works on the top floor of that building," Cam said, motioning to a high-rise office with rows of gleaming windows. "W.T. Diettich

& Associates. They're the fastest growing software manufacturer in the nation."

I shaded my eyes against the sun. "Impressive!"

He shrugged. "Right. But it still means going to the same old place day after day, being stuck behind the same old desk and working with the same people."

When he put it that way, I had to admit it didn't sound glamorous after all. At least my dad got to see lots of different patients each day—some even came from out-of-town to schedule appointments with him.

"I wish I'd brought my board along," Cam said wistfully, apparently eager to change the subject. We started walking again.

"Oh? You'd planned to skate here today?"

"I'd hoped to, but I guess thinking about the job sidetracked me."

"And getting held up at my folks' place probably didn't help either," I added with a chuckle.

He grinned, then paused and slanted me a questioning look. "You know about the skateboard park beneath the Burnside Bridge, don't you?"

"Uh-huh. I've overheard the skaters at school talk about it. They go there sometimes, I guess."

"Wanna check it out after we're done at New World Skates? If you've never seen it before, it's totally worth it."

"Of course I do!"

A couple of boys wearing baggy jeans and toting skateboards ducked into the store entrance just ahead. We followed them. Once inside, while Cam talked in the back room with the shop owner, I gazed in awe at the menagerie of colorful decks lining the walls: dragon-like creatures, skulls and cross-bones, insect mutations, even some with ribbons of fire like Cam's old board. What a sight! From the high ceiling hung a rainbow of windsocks and kits. Classical music filtered out through the sound system.

Several guys and a couple of girls milled about, peering into glass display cases or looking at new decks.

"First time here?" a girl with frizzy black hair and dangling earrings asked from behind the counter.

"Yeah, first time," I replied. From the loft-type workroom where someone was assembling a board, a drill whined.

I scanned the shop. "This place is cool."

"We've got the biggest mail-order business in the country," she said, pride edging her voice. "My uncle's the owner."

I gave her a quick once-over. She appeared to be about sixteen, and she wore black leggings and a crimson tunic top with a hip belt. She looked so sophisticated, so her own person. I couldn't help comparing her to some of the phony girls at school who thought they were cool with their artificial trendiness.

"What can I do for you?" she asked. "Show you a deck? Maybe some stickers?"

"Oh, no thanks! I'm just waiting for my boyfriend." *Boyfriend!* That was the first time I'd called Cam my boyfriend, and it sounded so good.

I drew in a breath, then asked, "Have you ever seen a deck with a butterfly on it?"

"Hmm. They're around, but a lot of them are custom made." I couldn't tell whether she was smiling to be friendly, or if she thought my butterfly idea sounded dumb. Judging from her sophisticated appearance, I decided on the latter. "Would you like me to look into ordering one for you?"

"Oh, no thanks. I can't afford a new board now anyway."

"We do have blank boards," she said.

"What?"

"Blank boards. It's a name for plain decks without graphics. They're a little cheaper, so new skaters often start out with them."

"I'm afraid that won't help me either," I said. I couldn't bring myself to tell her I was broke with a capital B. Thanks to my dear little sister.

She dismissed me with one last smile, then moved on down the counter.

"What's this I hear about decks with butterflies?" Cam asked from behind.

I spun around, wondering how long he'd been listening to our conversation. He looked down at me with a strange twinkle in his eyes, and I got that familiar quivery sensation inside.

"Oh, nothing." Despite my attempts to sound nonchalant, I wanted a new board so badly I could almost taste it.

"That was Tammy," Cam explained, darting a glance at the salesgirl. "She really knows her stuff when it comes to skateboards."

"I like her."

"Yeah, she reminds me of a girl I know in Santa Cruz. Talented, pretty, smart . . ."

I bit my lip. Why did Cam have to talk about other girls?

"Oh, don't get me wrong," he said, as if reading my thoughts. "She's my best buddy's girlfriend. Pee-Wee, we call her."

"Pee-Wee?" I bit back a smile.

"She's only four-eleven. We like to tease her about her height. Anyhow, Pee-Wee works at a skate shop in L.A. On the side, she does graphic artwork."

I knew it was silly, but I could feel jealousy eating inside of me. Somehow, it didn't matter if Pee-Wee *was* his best buddy's girlfriend. To make matters worse, he probably knew lots of girls in good old California.

"Chris and Pee-Wee are pretty tight," he went on. "They say when they get married, they're going to open their own skate shop, and then they can do exactly what they want to with it. The three of us used to hang together all the time."

"You miss them?" I asked.

He nodded, then changed the subject after a short pause. "Good news, Jessie! Guess what?"

I braced myself. "You got the job?"

"Yep, starting tomorrow." He beamed. "I have to report to work at nine forty-five."

"Congratulations!"

He grinned even wider. "Now we've got a *real* reason to celebrate."

I smacked my palm to my forehead in mock despair. "Oh, no! Not another celebration. I don't think I can take it."

"Sure you can. Let's go to Burnside!"

* * *

The rest of the day passed by much too quickly. After we left New World Skates, we crossed town and made our way to the skate park under the east side of the Burnside Bridge. I'd never seen so many skaters in one place before—and their aerials took my breath away. Cam pointed out two skaters that were performing front-side and back-side 180s—half rotations. I clutched my hands at my sides. *Yes! I'll do that someday too!* Other skaters carved the upper edge of a huge slope with such awesome agility, I felt all tingly inside just watching them. The energy surrounding us was so palpable, you could almost reach out and touch it. A crowd of onlookers had gathered to watch, and they clapped and cheered. Ecstatic, I joined in, raising my voice with theirs.

I felt reluctant when it was time to leave, but we still wanted to spend time at Waterfront Park, and already evening had settled over the city. Later, bundled in the warm jackets, we sat snuggled together on a park bench. The lights of the city reflected off the Willamette River like shimmering fireflies, and a tour boat paddled by. To our left, a bridge arched over the dark river. The scene appeared as if it had leapt right off the pages of a romance novel.

I snuggled in closer and lay my head on Cam's shoulder. Was it merely my imagination that I caught him sending me tender little glances? My emotions were on a crazy roller-coaster ride. One minute, as I remembered the lunchroom scene at school, new doubts crowed in. The next moment, I loved him so much, I refused to believe he was using me.

"I've had a terrific time today," I said with a sigh. "I'm so glad you got the job." I looked over at his perfectly chiseled profile, watched the night breeze ripple through his hair. He was even more gorgeous than the first time I'd seen him from the privacy of my room.

"Thanks. I'm glad too." He wrapped an arm around me, pulling me close. I could feel his breath fanning my forehead. Above us a flock of geese flew by in an arrow formation, their honking sounds fading into the noise of the traffic.

"Know something?" His voice broke through my reverie.

"Hmmm. What?"

"When we get that skate park in Preston—we will get it, you know—I'll be able to teach you some really rad tricks. There's nothing like the rush you get when you drop into a half-pipe or zoom off a twenty-foot slide."

"And what makes you so sure we'll get a skate park?" I asked, pulling away a little. If only I could let go of my doubts and be as positive as he was.

"Shh! Jessie, you ask too many questions." He drew me close again, then silently traced his finger down my cheek.

My heart sang as his lips pressed against mine.

Chapter Seven

The Christmas holidays and our usual two-week break from school passed with amazing speed. Though Cam was working steadily now at the skateboard shop and skated at Burnside on his lunch breaks, we somehow managed to be together every spare moment possible.

He continued to talk earnestly about the day Preston would build its own skate park. He never missed an opportunity to mention it to my father too. Dad only continued to shake his head and say Preston wasn't ready for that kind of undertaking. After all, the city budget had barely allowed for the reopening of the community swimming pool, and there were far more people who wanted to swim than skate.

Meanwhile, there'd been no further clues leading to the arrest of those responsible for the graffiti. To make matters worse, the culprits struck one more time—the very day we'd returned to school after New Years. Now, just when I'd figured the accusations had finally died down, they were flying all over town again.

The following Sunday, I took Megan to the store so she could see it too. She rode her bike, while I skated alongside of her. Thankfully, Cam had continued to loan me his spare board, but I was itching more-than-ever to finally get one of my own.

Her blue eyes narrowed as she stared at the latest scribbling. "I can't believe those guys had the nerve to come back and do it again. As if the first time wasn't bad enough."

"I agree." I thought about what the reporter had said. "As far as the people around here are concerned, we are the bad guys every time. "

A line of oak tress behind the store thrust tortuous bare branches into the gray January sky. I pulled out my lip balm from my jacket pocket and ran it over my dry lips.

"Well, if anyone asks my opinion, I'll stick up for you," Megan said. "You and Cam and Pete and all the rest." Lately, she'd been hanging out with our crowd, watching us practice on the mini-ramp in Pete's front yard.

My friend chewed on her lower lip, apparently lost in thought. "Did anyone see the kids last night? Is there any evidence it's the same kids that lady said she saw the *first* time?"

"According to Dad, they got away completely unnoticed. The only evidence is that yesterday half this wall was covered with graffiti. Now there's twice as much." I shivered against the cold. The air smelled fresh as it often does before snowfall.

We were in no hurry to move on, so we sat down on the sidewalk in front of the store.

Megan pulled her pink knit ski cap down over her ears and broke into a smile. "Did I tell you? Pete asked me out for pizza tonight."

"No way! That's awesome." I was certain if they started dating, he'd get her interested in skating too. Then I wouldn't be the only girl skater in Preston.

After we discussed the movie they were planning to see, a new sci-fi flick that everyone was raving about, we changed the subject to Cam—and I shared my mixed-up feelings with my friend. My love for him was growing all the time. I'd convinced myself that he must love me too, although he'd only said he *liked* me that one time soon after we'd met. Megan had been sympathetic, a terrific listener. Yet Cam was *my* problem, and I'd have to deal with it myself.

Standing up to leave, we wandered towards a vacant parking lot that stood between the store and a sprawling brick church. The wheels of Megan's bike squeaked as I ambled next to her, my skateboard in hand.

From the opened church doors, a flood of people emerged. I could hear talking and laughter.

"Ever been inside that church?" she asked, her gaze following mine.

"Yeah, just a few weeks ago on Christmas Eve with my Uncle Burt," I answered. My favorite uncle always spent the holidays with us. That night, the sight of the richly-colored stained-glass windows and flickering candles had filled me with a warm, happy feeling.

A gray-haired priest appeared on the front steps.

"That's Fr. O'Riley," I said. A few snowflakes began sifting down, icy and feather-like against my cheeks. "Dad's talked a lot about his work in the community, helping to improve the housing conditions for the migrant workers. He used to be a carpenter before he went into the priesthood, I guess."

"Yeah, I've read about him in the paper."

The priest started walking our way. Was he going to yell at us too? Tell me to take my skateboard and leave?

"Good day, ladies," he said. I was taken aback by his friendly manner. In fact, he reminded me a lot of Uncle Burt, and I liked that.

"Hey," we chorused.

"My name's Fr. O'Riley." He had a round, jolly face and kind blue eyes that crinkled at the corners when he smiled.

"I met you on Christmas Eve," I said respectfully. After introducing him to Megan, I reminded him of my name.

"Yes, of course, I remember you. Your father's a mighty good man, my dear. I've been a devoted supporter."

"Thanks. I had to admit, I couldn't help feeling even more proud of Dad."

His gaze drifted past us. "I see you girls have been admirin' our recently acquired artwork. Really somethin', isn't it?"

I shifted my weight from one foot to the other. "Uh-huh, it's awful, all right."

He shook his head. "I suppose next people will start defacing churches too. Such a pity."

I couldn't hold back any longer. "Honest, Fr. O'Riley, my friends and I—we're skateboarders—but we didn't do it! I swear!"

He held up his hand. "Now did I say that? Anyone could be responsible, eh? I have faith in today's young people. It's not right that folks blame our youth for everything that's wrong on this old planet."

"You really mean that?" I blurted.

A slow smile crept across his face. "I'm a priest. I can't go about town accusin' folks of something I'm not sure about. And yes, I do have faith in the new generation."

"But Fr. O'Riley," I asked, "how can we prove to the rest of the town we didn't do it?"

He ran his hand over his chin and stared at the ground. "Now that's a tough one. You'll have to start in small ways. Little stepping stones."

"Meaning?" Megan asked.

He paused, scratching his head. "Meaning perhaps you can start things moving in the right direction. Paint over the graffiti. Clean it up right. The store owner's a busy man, and I know he'd appreciate the help."

I felt my defenses beginning to melt like the snowflakes striking my warm cheeks.

"Yes, maybe we can do that. I know my boyfriend, Cam, would want to say yes too."

With a nod, he reached into his breast pocket and pulled out a business card. "The man you need to see is Harry Crosham. He gave me his card yesterday when he was here to inspect the damage."

I gulped. "Mr. Crosham? The one who owns the hardware store?" Visions of a crabby old man glaring at Angie and me from beneath a dimly-lit porch light marched by me.

"Right. He's a very successful businessman and owns a lot of property in town. You must call him."

I wasn't so sure Mr. Crosham would welcome our help as much as the priest had said, but I took the card anyway and stuck it in my pocket.

"And young ladies . . ." Megan and I exchanged anxious glances as we waited for him to continue.

"Let me know whenever you get started, all right? I'd like to give you and your friends a hand. That is, if you'll let me."

I broke into a grin. "Sure! Of course, we'll let you." Though it was the dead of winter, I felt as if warm spring sunshine had flooded over me.

It was obvious Fr. O'Riley was on our side.

* * *

"Just think of all the money I've saved!" Angie chirped at me the following evening. We were ambling through the Lakecrest Mall, window shopping, while Mom got a cut and color at the beauty salon.

I groaned. "Yeah, I bet it's tons more than I've managed to save. Am I ever glad our agreement's finally over." It'd amazed me she hadn't spent the entire amount by then.

At least my bribery had worked. Ever since our agreement, whenever Cam called or stopped by, Angie had been the picture of cooperation. But now that Christmas was over, would I have to dream up something new?

I slanted her a glance. "How much have you saved?"

"Forty-five dollars and thirty-eight cents," she proclaimed. "Enough to buy lots of earrings."

"I think Mom and Dad would like it better if you saved your money for something constructive, as they'd say."

"What are you saving your money for?" she wanted to know.

With a sigh, I told her about my plans for a new skateboard. "Thanks to you," I added, "I've a long way to go."

We approached the This&That Shop, the place where they sold all sorts of accessories.

"Oh, please, Jessie! Let's go in there. It won't be long now till I get my ears pierced, and I want to look for a pair of long dangly earrings to go with my new dress."

I remembered the eclectic assortment we'd looked at earlier in the department store at the end of the mall. Cheesy gold earrings that hung almost to her belly-button, a pair of huge neon yellow earrings that reminded me of two garish light bulbs. What a kid! She was trying so hard to be sophisticated.

"Okay," I said. "We'll go inside and see what looks good. We have almost an hour till it's time to meet Mom outside the food court, so we've still got some time to kill."

Soft jazz drifted from the sound system as we strolled inside the store. Clusters of teenage girls hovered over display cases. A few girls about Angie's age were lined up to purchase their treasures.

It was tempting to tell my sister she was wasting her money, but I knew it was useless. Besides, in my heart of hearts—and I hadn't told my folks yet, not even Cam—I'd been planning on getting a butterfly tattoo on my ankle. My parents would probably say that was a waste of money too.

We wended our way through the narrow aisles to the earring counter.

"Look at these!" Angie snatched a pair of diamond-shaped purple earrings and held them up to her face. "What do you think? Do they go with my complexion? Do they match my eyes?"

I giggled. "Oh, sure. Since when did you sprout purple eyes?"

She appeared to ignore my teasing. "Too bad Cam doesn't have any younger brothers."

"Why?" I watched her smile at herself in a nearby three-way mirror.

"I already told you. I like Cam. But he's too old for me." She paused then flashed me an impish smile. "I wish he had a brother that was about my age."

I reached down and ruffled her hair. "Sis, you're really something!"

Chapter Eight

"Hey, knock it off!" I burst into laughter. "You're plastering me with paint!" Cam looked innocently ahead, dabbing the last few needed strokes of cream-colored paint against the outside south store wall. "Sure, sure. Now why would I do a thing like that?"

"Just to give me a bad time, that's why," I replied, laughing so hard now my sides hurt. "I hope Mr. Crosham has lots of paint remover," I added, "because I'm a total mess!" I peered down at my smudged hands. Thank goodness, I'd decide to wear one of dad's large flannel shirts over my jeans and sweater. At the last minute, I'd retrieved it from the box of clothing we'd set aside to take to the Goodwill.

After school the following day, Cam, Megan, and I dashed over to the old store to get started painting again. The other kids said they'd join us later. If we didn't waste time, we'd have a couple of hours of daylight left.

Though I'd been nervous about approaching Mr. Crosham the day before, he was much nicer than I'd expected. Not only had he provided us with plenty of paint and extra brushes, he'd also offered to pay each of us fifty dollars. Thinking about all the baby-sitting money I'd forked over to my sis, I'd jumped at the opportunity.

Now as I stroked more paint onto the wall, I caught sight of Fr. O'Riley walking in our direction. I waved, and he waved back. He was dressed in a plaid wool shirt and baggy jeans, and he carried a couple of paint brushes. Once we were face-to-face, I made quick introductions.

"You kids have saved Harry a lot of work," the priest said. "I know he appreciates that, though he sometimes doesn't show it."

"Fifty bucks for two hours of work isn't too bad," Cam said. He flicked a water-soaked paint brush in my direction and sent me a disarming smile. "Pretty soon we'll be rolling in big bucks."

"But that's not all!" I exclaimed. I told Fr. O'Riley about Cam's job at New World Skates, emphasizing what a pro he was. While we were painting and talking, Pete and Andy arrived. Soon Nick and three other skaters I didn't know had joined us too. Everyone was eager to get the job done, and Fr. O'Riley seemed pleased about that.

After we worked for a while, the priest put down his brush and asked, "Mind if I ask a favor, eh?"

"Of course not," I replied.

"I'd like to try to skate."

You could've knocked me over with a kitten's whisker. I couldn't find the words to answer him.

"Sure! Take my board!" Pete exclaimed from off to the side where he'd been listening.

The priest tossed a glance over his shoulder towards the empty churchyard and grinned. "Just don't tell any of my congregation. A priest is supposed to be proper, if you know what I mean."

We all laughed. Fr. O'Riley was right—he was certainly different from any priest I'd ever known.

He placed one foot on the board and began pumping furiously with the other foot. "Hold on world, here I come!" Though the incline was only a gentle one, it was enough to give him momentum. Soon all we could see was his backside and his flailing arms and hands.

"Oh, no! He's gonna crash!" Andy exclaimed.

"He's way too old for this," Cam said under his breath.

In seconds the priest righted himself, made a wide U-turn, and zoomed back towards us. We breathed a collective sigh of relief.

"Hey, way to go!" Pete yelled.

"Not bad, Fr. O'Riley," Megan said. "You should skate more often!"

The priest twisted his face into a wry smile. "Agreed, my dear. Maybe with a little more practice, I'll catch on." He stopped talking, then laughed heartily. "Can't you just hear the talk around town? Small town priest turns skateboarder." He handed the board back to Pete and continued, "I can remember back in the old days when skateboarding first got started. A typical board wasn't much more than an old crate on roller skates."

"Did you skate then?" I asked.

"No, but the thought crossed my mind a time or two." He straightened his shirt. "That reminds me. There was something I planned to mention, and I guess there's no time like the present."

"What?" we chorused.

"I assume, accordin' to everything I've heard, that you kids are havin' a hard time findin' a place to skate."

"You can say *that* again." I answered for all of us. I didn't want to tell him that Mr. Crosham was one of our biggest problems.

"How'd you like to use the church parkin' lot durin' off-hours?" he asked. "If you have ramps, bring them. You can even build a half-pipe down on the end where no one goes."

I gasped. "Wow! You really mean that?"

"You've got to be kidding!" Andy said with a grin.

"Well now, you want I should say it's all a big joke?" His dark eyes danced beneath bushy white eyebrows.

"Oh, Fr. O'Riley!" I cried. "Thanks! Thanks a bunch." I darted a sidelong look at Cam and saw the happiness shining in his eyes. Soon we were all talking and laughing. I wanted to pinch myself to make sure it was for real. At last our problems were over!

* * *

"What's going on?" Cam asked the following Saturday. Dad had escorted him into our family room where Angie and I'd been playing Clue and arguing about whose turn it was to unload the dishwasher.

I grinned up at him and got that familiar little thrill running down my spine. "Oh, just another sisterly squabble." Even though most of the commotion at our house had ended two months earlier, I hadn't forgotten her telling me how she'd felt left out. I was trying hard to be more patient with Angie.

"You got back early?" I asked, glancing at the clock in the hallway.

"Yep. Things were kind of slow, so the boss said to take off." He was smiling mysteriously, but before I could ask why, Angie started yammering as usual.

"Cam, wanna see my school picture? Come on! Pretty please? It's in my room."

"Sure, kiddo, but first give me five!" He held out his hand while she smacked it hard.

"Oh! You're a strong little thing, aren't you?" He waved his hand about as if to cool it off, all the while smiling crookedly and feigning discomfort.

"Surprised you, huh?" She grinned like a Cheshire cat.

I shook my head as he trailed behind her into her room. "You two better make it snappy!" I exclaimed with mock sternness. "I'm not waiting forever."

In a short while, he appeared again—without Angie. In the background, I could hear her talking on the phone.

"So are you ready to go?" Cam asked.

I blinked. "Go where?"

"Hello, Cam!" Mom breezed past us carrying a cardboard box.

"Hey, Mrs. Williams."

She dumped the box onto the closest chair and rubbed her hands together. "I was out in the garage, gathering up extra boxes. Next weekend's the big rummage sale at the community center, and I've got to get some things organized."

Poor Mom, I thought as I squeezed back my annoyance over still another interruption. Now that she didn't have Dad's campaign to organize, she apparently had to dream up something else. Her life was the same way with everything separated into neat little compartments. *Good thing I don't take after her.*

After she'd vanished out of sight, I looked again at Cam and repeated, "Okay, so where are we going?"

"To the church!"

"The church?"

"Yes! The lumber's here." His voice bubbled with eagerness. "The delivery guy dropped it off in the parking lot a little while ago. I've already talked to Fr. O'Riley, and he's given us the green light to get started building the half-pipe!"

"But I don't get it. *What* lumber? And when did this all happen?"

"I told my folks about the priest and the parking lot and the half-pipe. They said they wanted to help, so they put in an order for the lumber this morning." He brushed a lock of hair off his forehead. "And if everything goes right, I should have enough money saved up to pay them back in a couple of weeks."

"This is unreal! Things are happening even faster than I'd imagined."

He gave me a tender kiss, then clasped my hand and led me to the hall coat closet. "Grab a warm jacket. You might need it."

Although my knees were still wobbly from his kiss, I managed to paw through the closet and shrug into my fleece-line denim jacket.

"Your parents are really generous," I told him after we'd driven away in the Mercedes. "I mean, getting all that lumber together for us and all." Hiding my smile, I noticed some biscuit-colored paint streaked against his blond hair. He stopped at a cross-walk while two kids about Angie's age sauntered by.

"Fr. O'Riley says he's got saws, hammers, and anything else we might need in his rectory," Cam said.

"He's been a big help already," I mused aloud. "I like his attitude. He thinks skating's cool and we're worthwhile."

"He's not the only one," Cam pointed out. "Take Mr. Crosham, for instance. And your dad."

I had to admit—regardless of Cam's presumed motives—he was right. Maybe there was hope for Preston yet.

After we arrived at the church parking lot, I jumped out of the car and sniffed the smell of the freshly-cut plywood. Excitement flowed through me. I'd never built a thing in my life before, not even a birdhouse like Angie made at camp last summer, but I was willing to give it my best shot.

Cam looked down at me. I detected a glimmer of tenderness in his eyes, deep misty pools of green that I could almost get lost in.

"We've got our work cut out for us," he muttered, grazing my cheek with his hand.

"I bet it's going to take weeks to get the half-pipe done."

"The longer the better."

"What?" Was he out of his mind? "I thought you were the one who couldn't wait."

"Yes and no." He grinned. "I figure if I can hold onto you long enough till we get this thing done, then maybe—just maybe—you'll keep sticking around."

At a loss for words, I studied his face. Hold onto *me*? Did he mean that? More than anything, I wanted to believe him, but my doubts kept getting in the way. Changing the subject, I pulled back and asked, "So where's Fr. O'Riley? How do we get started?"

Cam dug into his pocket and produced a piece of folded graph paper. "He should be along any second now. When I talked with him earlier, I showed him these rough plans I got at New World Skates. He thought they looked excellent, and I'm really stoked that he's supporting us this way."

I stared down at a penciled sketch of the half-pipe, and my veins thrummed with anticipation. "I can't believe it! It's really happening."

"Believe it. It's for real! Fr. O'Riley suggested we build it in three parts," he continued, tracing the lines with his index finger. "The middle is here at the bottom and the two raised sections are on either end. That way, if we ever have to, it'll be a lot easier to move to another spot."

"Good idea. Who else is going to help us?"

"Pete, Randy, Nick, and a few others. Pete said Megan wanted to come, but she's studying for a test."

I laughed. "Be glad. Knowing Megan, she'd spend more time hitting her thumb with the hammer than getting any work done." I glanced over at the south side of the old grocery store. In the late afternoon grayness, I could see our clean, newly-painted wall. It gave me a good feeling inside. Even if Mr. Crosham hadn't offered to pay us for our work, it would've been worth it just cleaning up that mess.

Soon the other kids arrived. For the next couple of hours we measured and sawed and hammered and measured again as if our lives depended on it—Fr. O'Riley included. At last, trying to work in near-total darkness, we had to rely on a make-shift spotlight the priest had rigged up for us.

"I can hardly wait for the first time I drop into this half-pipe," Andy said above the whine of the power saw.

"Yeah, and it'll be cool carving the edges," Nick agreed. "I plan to work on my front side nose slides and 5-0 grinds."

I sat down on a sawhorse and let out an audible sigh.

Andy grinned. "You look wiped out."

I pulled a face. "So what if I am? Have you heard me complaining?"

My hands tingled and my back ached. Still, it felt wonderful to know that when the half-pipe was finally finished, we'd have a place to skate that was safe and legal. Already the broad U-shaped foundation was looking good.

Fr. O'Riley straightened, rubbing his back, then nodded towards the small house where he lived next to the church. "Let's call it a night, okay? I ordered three big pizzas, just waitin' inside. Anyone hungry?"

"Yes!" we shouted in unison while Nick and Pete pumped fists into the air. A few minutes later we hurried inside and gathered around a cozy woodstove in the front room. I closed my eyes and allowed my thoughts to drift as the inviting warmth wrapped around me.

Cam's voice jerked me from my reverie. "Darn! I think I left my wallet on the saw horse. I'll be right back."

"Wait," I said. "I'll go with you."

Fr. O'Riley handed Cam a flashlight. "Here. This might come in handy."

We hurried back outside. Cam beamed the flashlight on the sawhorse and said, "At least it's still—"

Footsteps pounded from somewhere close by. As I whirled around and peered in the direction of the old store, I gasped.

Shadowy figures were vanishing into the night.

Chapter Nine

"Cam! Look! Over there!"

Beneath a pool of streetlight that illuminated the wall of the old store, we gaped at the newly-applied spray paint. New graffiti was plastered from one end to the other.

My hands shook. "They're getting away!"

"Oh, no, they aren't!" he said hotly. He tore out after them.

"Wait! I'm coming too!"

"Go back inside the rectory," Cam hollered to me.

"No, I want to help!" Already Cam was about a hundred feet ahead of me. It looked as if he might even catch up with them, but then what? A shudder zipped through me.

The cold winter air smarted my eyes as I raced ahead, dodging an old tire someone had dumped in the middle of the parking lot. Skateboards clattered behind me. I glanced over my shoulder. Pete and Nick must've heard our shouts. They were approaching, quickly gaining ground.

I rounded the north side of the store. Looking past Cam, I caught sight of three figures, two short bulky frames, the other tall and lanky. My head thudded.

Instantly they piled into a white van parked next to a dumpster.

I stopped in my tracks as the van lunged forward. Wheels screeched. The smell of burning rubber filled the air. Seconds later, the van swerved to the right and careened out onto the highway.

"I got their license." Cam sprinted back to where we stood waiting. "Those dudes weren't too smart, leaving their van parked under a streetlight. I was just close enough to see. Help me remember it, Jessie." He rattled the number off effortlessly.

"Got it!" I repeated it back to him.

"This sucks!" Pete said. "If the cops can't track down these jerks now, they never will!"

Cam's jaw tensed. "I'll head straight over to the police station."

While the rest of the kids put away the tools in the storage shed, Cam and I took off. Sergeant McFarland, a stock middle-aged patrolman, scowled as he listened to our story. After what'd seemed like an eternity, he finished entering his report into his computer. "I'll get on it immediately," he said. Then he disappeared through the back door.

"Fr. O'Riley said if you need any more eye witnesses, just give him a call!" I yelled after him. I doubted whether he'd heard me.

I shrugged. Though I was exhausted, waves of optimism washed over me. Maybe—at last—we'd know the truth! It was time the people of Preston stopped blaming us for something we hadn't done.

Back at the rectory, where the others were still munching on pizza and drinking soft drinks, I collapsed onto a floral printed couch next to Cam. The spicy smells of pepperoni pizza wafted in from the kitchen, and in the background, I heard music playing.

"What happened at the police station?" Andy asked. "Are the cops going to arrest them?"

"The chances look good," Cam answered. "Getting that license plate number was really our ace in the hole."

After the conversation had drifted off to talk about the try-outs at school for *Our Town*, I rested my head on Cam's shoulder and sighed. "Wow, what a night. I'm tired."

"Me too," he murmured. "Tired *and* hungry."

After we'd both scarfed down a few slices of pizza, I looked over at the priest. It was obvious, despite still another spray-painting incident a while earlier, he was enjoying our company.

"Fr. O'Riley?" I asked.

"Yes, my dear?"

"Why are you doing this? Going out of your way to be so nice to us, I mean."

His eyes took on a far-away look. "I may seem old to you, but I'm not too old to remember my own youth. Back when I was a kid growin' up in a little town in Wisconsin, I owned a motorcycle. A dirt bike, to be exact. That's what I really loved to do—tear around the countryside, feeling the warmth of the sun on my face and the wind rushing past me. So did a few of my best buddies. We couldn't be on the highways, of course, so we found old roads in a deserted pasture. But soon the farmers started to complain. 'No good hoods' they said. 'Nothin' but a bunch of hell-raisers. They're scarin' our cows, raisin' too much dust, and destroyin' our peace and quiet.'"

As we talked, I leaned forward, eager to catch every word. Already I was beginning to understand.

"We didn't mean to bother them, or their cows," he continued with a wry chuckle. "We simply wanted to have fun. But soon we found ourselves as branded as the cattle in their pastures. To them, motor cycling and delinquency practically went hand-in-hand."

"So what did you do?" Pete asked. "Did you have to get rid of your bikes?"

"Fortunately not. An elderly couple who liked kids and owned several acres of untended pasture decided to act. They hired a bulldozer which carved out miles of trails for us. What a red-letter day when we finally were allowed to take our bikes onto their land. I'll never forget that old man and woman for as long as I live."

"So what you're saying is that you were misunderstood too?" Cam asked. "You know how that feels."

"Yes. But it goes far beyond misunderstandin'. It's really a story about knowin' someone out there believes in you. Someone who is willin' to stand up and say, 'Take another look, folks. You've got it all wrong. These kids are worth it.'"

My throat tightened. "And now you're doing the same thing for us."

"That's right. Maybe now I can pay it forward."

Deeply touched, I thought about his story. Some day when I was grown up and living in an exciting foreign country, I'd have an opportunity to crusade against prejudice and narrow-mindedness too.

But who knew? Perhaps the opportunity would happen here in my own backyard. Maybe I wouldn't have to travel to the far corners of the world to make a difference.

Pete's voice yanked me out of my thoughts. "I sure hope those jerks don't mess around with our half-pipe," he said. He bit into his pepperoni pizza and lifted a shoulder. "I don't trust them one bit. And what I don't get is this—why can't Preston catch up with the times? I mean, skateboarding is highly respected in the rest of the world. It might have taken a while, but boarding is even part of the Winter Olympics now, not to mention the X games."

"You got it, man," Nick put in.

"I'll keep an eye on the half-pipe," Fr. O'Riley said. He folded his hands in his lap. "That's a promise."

"Did the van look familiar?" I turned to Andy who'd lived in Preston for nearly as long as I had.

"Nope. Not at all. I'm sure they were outsiders."

"Ditto," Pete agreed with a scowl. "They had to be from out-of-town. I've never seen a van like that around here before."

"Don't sweat it," Cam said. "Like I told Jessie at the police station, I know we'll catch up with them. I just have this feeling."

My heart sank. He might be feeling hopeful, but somehow I wasn't anymore. Maybe I was just too tired to think clearly now.

That night as I tried to sleep, I kept thinking about Fr. O'Riley's story and how he was helping us. Thoughts of the kids in the white van also churned in my brain. What if the police discovered the van had been stolen? What if they never tracked down the identity of the driver and his buddies? All the what ifs kept swimming around in my head, nearly driving me crazy.

During the next few weekends, every chance we could get, we worked on our half-pipe. Although Cam wasn't there most of the time, I enjoyed hanging with the other skaters. Yet my best time of the day was when Cam finally arrived in the late afternoons. I so admired him. After working his shifts at New World Skates, he never complained.

Even Mr. Crosham stopped by a time or two. He seemed to enjoy giving us a few pointers, and of course, we promised we'd help him again by painting over the latest graffiti.

"I'll pay you kids double this time," he'd offered with a hearty chuckle. "After all, if it wasn't for your spotting the suspects, we'd still be at square one."

The more I got to know the older man, the more I realized how nice he really was. Although he had chased Cam and the other skaters out of his parking lot in the beginning, I now regretted any snap judgments I might have made about him.

Finally, a week later, good news arrived! Cam received a call from the police department saying they'd tracked down the name of the owner of the white van: a nineteen-year-old kid from Portland. And he *wasn't* a skateboarder! He and his buddies confessed to all three incidences at the old Safeway. They were arrested and socked with a huge fine, plus one-hundred hours of community service.

To my relief, there was even a long article about it in the local paper. The piece glowingly praised the skaters for cleaning up the graffiti, quoting Mr. Crosham. It was about time our good deeds went public! I promised myself I'd thank Mr. Crosham for his comments the next time I saw him.

On Friday after school, Fr. O'Riley called me and asked, "Jessica, dear, can you come over to my office in the church? Soon?"

"Of course, but what's wrong?" There was no mistaking the concern in his voice.

"We'll talk about it when you get here. Bring Cam along too, if possible."

"Sure. He's supposed to stop by any minute now. We'll be right over."

After Cam arrived, I blurted out Fr. O'Riley's request. "He sounds worried or upset about something. Says we'll talk about it after we get to his office."

Cam's face clouded. "Suppose it's something to do with the kids in the white van? Maybe they came back and trashed our half-pipe, just like we were worried might happen."

My mouth went dry. "I hope not! Come on, the suspense is killing me."

After leaving Mom a note, we raced across the street to Cam's house and sped off to the church. In minutes we'd arrived.

"I'm afraid I have unfavorable news," Fr. O'Riley said to us from behind his oversized oak desk. He frowned and little worry-lines wrinkled his brow. "Three days ago I got a call from the bishop of California."

"A call?" I asked.

"Yes, the man's name is Bishop Shaw. There's a dire need in the southern farmin' areas to set up migrant camps. How many, I'm not sure, though I hear the situation is critical. Bishop Shaw says he must have someone to fill it immediately. I'm the only one he feels is qualified."

I gripped the sides of my chair. "You mean to say you're leaving us?"

His gaze dropped. "I'm afraid so. Next week. I'm goin' to miss this community dreadfully—you kids especially. But I'll only be one state away, you know. I want you to send me an e-mail or letter now and again to let me know how you're gettin' on."

"We will," Cam said, swallowing repeatedly. He hesitated. "But can't you say no?"

Fr. O'Riley rearranged a stack of papers on his desk as if pondering what to say next. From the belfry of the church, the chimes struck five. "I'm afraid not. At my ordination, I took solemn vows of obedience. I'm obligated. There's no turning back." His voice broke. "But that's only the first part. I'm afraid there's more bad news."

"What?" Cam asked, apprehension etched on his face.

Yes, what? I silently cried. *What could be worse than losing Fr. O'Riley?*

"The new priest who's takin' my place, Fr. Malcom, is a wonderful man. Dedicated. Reliable. And from the old school, so to speak. I've talked to him about our agreement and the half-pipe we've been buildin.'"

My head whirled. I couldn't bear to hear what was coming.

"Unfortunately, he doesn't agree with me," Fr. O'Riley continued. "He thinks the half-pipe will get in the way, be a nuisance to the parishioners. He's askin' that you take it down, find another place to finish it." He bit his lip. "I'm afraid I couldn't change his mind, no matter how hard I tried. I'm sorry, kids. Dreadfully sorry."

"That sucks," Cam said.

I nodded silently.

"Yeah, it does suck," the priest replied. "Again, I'm sorry. So very sorry."

Cam took my hand, giving it a quick squeeze. "Don't apologize, Fr. O'Riley. We hate the thought of your leaving, but you're doing the right thing. And for us—" He shrugged. "Somehow it will all work out."

"You're right, young man. It will work out. I know you kids will find a place to skate—a permanent place. And before long, the citizens of Preston, instead of criticizing, will come from miles around to admire your skills." His expectant gaze slid from Cam to me. "You *do* believe that, eh?"

"Well, sort of." I twisted the hem of my sweater. "But what makes you so sure?" I couldn't help wondering whether he'd received a private message from God that we weren't privy to.

His mouth turned up in a half smile. "Remember when I said we older folks must have faith in the new generation? Well, I've got faith in you. You've already taken the first step, my dear, in showin' your willingness to clean up the graffiti to keep our town a good place to live." He turned to Cam and smiled wider. "I like your industriousness. You kids are the stuff winners are made of. You'll find your way, I know."

I jumped up from my chair and hugged him. I felt his strong arms wrapped around me, hugging me back. Tears smarted my eyes.

"Thanks. We're going to miss you, Fr. O'Riley," I murmured. "*A lot.*"

Chapter Ten

Before I realized it, Valentine's Day had arrived. Cam surprised me with a big heart-shaped box filled with milk chocolates, and I gave him a homemade card complete with butterflies and hearts. He'd kissed me and said it was the best Valentine card he'd ever received. More than anything, I wanted to believe it. How many other girls had slipped him romantic Valentine messages in the past? It must've been tons.

I'd also received a lacy red-and-white card from Fr. O'Riley with a note tucked inside. It was the third time I'd heard from him since he'd moved away. With the card he included a detailed sketch that made me laugh. It portrayed an image of him dressed in his black cassock, tearing down a hill on a skateboard.

To Jessie, my dear, he wrote. *As always, many thanks for your emails. I think of you kids all the time. My new ministry is working out well. Not only have we nearly completed a large dorm-type facility for the migrant families, we've drawn up blue prints for a mission here. Keep in touch, okay? Give my love to Cam and all your friends.*

As I read his letter, thoughts of our disassembled half-pipe popped into my head. For the past few weeks, we'd been storing it in Cam's backyard. What a waste, I thought gloomily every time I looked at it. Cam worked so hard to earn that money—and he'd paid back his parents every cent. Though I knew he loved his job, it bothered me when I couldn't be with him.

The following Monday morning as we wandered through the crowded hallway at school towards the cafeteria, I showed him Fr. O'Riley's letter.

After reading it and admiring the sketch, he laughed as hard as I had when I'd first seen it. "I've been thinking a lot about what the priest told us before he left town," Cam said, sobering a little.

"About the skate park?"

"Uh-huh." He narrowed his eyes as if remembering that terrible day we'd learned the priest was leaving. "Fr. O'Riley's right. We've got to show we're willing to work for what we want, that we'll hold up our end of the deal."

We filed through the salad bar line, heaping our plates with lettuce and an assortment of other veggies.

"But how?" I asked. The sounds of clanking dishes floated in from the kitchen.

"By first convincing city hall that the need for a skate park exists. Then we'll have to draw up a plan, a proposal that'll knock them off their feet." He waved a hand enthusiastically.

"That sounds like more work than building the half-pipe!" I said.

"It *will* be more work, but we can do it. I swear we can."

As we skirted past Mike and Rocky and sat down at a table, I noticed them staring in our direction. Rocky's laughing dark eyes seemed to mock me.

I lifted my chin and looked the other way. Their stupid accusations about Cam were wrong, dead wrong. I'd finally come to my senses and realized that. Cam was simply too honest. Too sincere. Too wonderful in every way. He'd never use anybody.

"You know them?" Cam asked. Obviously he'd never had the good fortune of having any classes with Preston's two top jocks.

"Sort of. But don't worry, they're not my type."

"And I'm your type?" he asked, his eyes twinkling.

I tweaked his arm. "What do you think?"

He shot me an answering grin. Pure joy flowed over me. There'd never be anyone for me but Cam.

"So back to our proposal," I said. "Let's try to catch Megan and Pete and everyone right after school. We'll do some brainstorming before we put it down on paper."

"Now you're talking!" Cam's voice rung with approval. He cut open his bagel and began spreading cream cheese on it. "It wouldn't hurt to discuss this with your dad before the meeting. We'll want to make sure there's plenty of room for us on the agenda."

I nodded in agreement, mentally mapping out the best plan of attack.

"When are the city council meetings?" Cam asked.

"Umm, the first Thursday of every month, I think. I'll check with Dad."

Cam took a big gulp of milk, then wiped his mouth with the back of his hand. "Good. That gives us time to get organized. After we meet with the others, would you like to come over to my place so we can nail it all down?" He flashed me a smile. "After all, it's a lot quieter at my house than yours."

"Sure." I smiled back. "I couldn't agree more."

* * *

My breath caught as I walked down the hallway inside Cam's house and paused to peek inside the sunny parlor. It looked like a palace: thick wine-colored Persian rugs, a stately grand piano in the corner, and his mother's collection of intricate-patterned china and hand-carved figurines in a big oak hutch. It was such a contrast to the everyday hodge-podge at my house. Early Marriage, my mother always referred to it, noting the well-used furniture she and Dad had purchased almost two decades earlier. It's not that we couldn't afford newer stuff; it's just that when Mom gets attached to something, she holds onto it forever.

"Let's work at the dining room table," Cam said, jolting me out of my thoughts. "I've already set up my laptop there."

"Where do we start?" I asked a minute later after we'd wandered into the dining room.

"First sit down!" He chuckled.

I plopped down in one of the two empty chairs closest to us. He sat, too, and didn't hesitate to reach for my hand. Then he drew me closer and kissed me, slowly and deeply. The thrill that shot through me made my toes curl.

"Hmmm, I think *this* is where we should start," he said, tucking back a lock of my hair behind my ear. "That was nice, Jessie." He pulled back with obvious reluctance.

"Only problem is, we won't get any work done this way, will we?" I straightened, too, and cleared my throat. Oh, how I wanted to keep kissing him.

"Unfortunately not." One corner of his mouth turned up in a smile. "Okay, here's the plan," he went on. "Number one, we've got to sort through the results of our brainstorming this afternoon. Decide what to use and what to throw out. Number two will involve a little research."

I wrinkled my nose. "Research! This is getting to sound disgustingly a lot like that stupid Study Skills class I had to take last year. The one old Mr. Ruskins taught."

He held up a finger, imitating the teacher's monotonous drone. "Pardon the correction, Jessica, my dear, but the word is *teaches*. The infamous B.J. Ruskins still *teaches* his infamous course. You've apparently forgotten I'm his prized student."

"Okay, okay—*teaches*!"

I broke into hysterics. "Oh, Cam, you're too much."

The corners of his mouth twitched, but he maintained his even gaze. "Now back to our work."

"Of course. Bring it on!" The mouth-watering fragrance of something baking in the oven drifted from the kitchen. He leaned a little closer, fiddling with his pen. He smelled like fresh air and toothpaste. "Next step, we'll have to appoint committees. One to look into a location, one to determine sources of financing, one to check out stuff like liability insurance and maintenance. You get the idea. In other words, it's going to take a lot of people."

I groaned. "That's a tall order for sure! But the biggest part is money, right?"

"Exactly. That'll be everyone's first concern. Where will it come from? The city budget? Fundraisers? Donations from the community?"

For the next hour or so, Cam and I busied ourselves drawing up plans for committees and decided the best way to get a task force organized. It was mind-boggling!

Cam's mother appeared carrying a tray filled with brownies and two glasses of milk. "Here's some nourishment for when the going gets rough," she said with a wink, setting the plate between us. Her green eyes, so much like Cam's, smiled down at us. I was glad she hadn't seen us kissing a few minutes earlier—or had she?

"Thanks, Mom." Cam offered me a brownie, then grabbed a handful for himself. He opened a file on his computer. His brow creased, as if he were deep in thought.

"So what are you seeing there—?"

The phone in the hallway rang, cutting my question short. "Ah, I think I'd better take this one," Cam said. Darting me an apologetic glance, he asked, "You don't mind, do you, Jessie?"

"Of course not. Go for it!"

He got to his feet. *I'll only be a minute*, he mouthed to me as he started towards the phone.

I nodded and smiled. A few minutes passed. Waiting patiently, I bit into another brownie and savored each rich chocolately mouthful.

Cam didn't return. I stood up from the table and stretched my muscles. I wandered about the dining room, looking at nothing in particular. *What time is it?* I wondered, then checked my watch. Nine fifty-five. Pretty soon I'd need to go home.

Unexpectedly, I caught sight of an envelope—an opened envelope—lying on the side table. It was addressed to Cam in delicately flowing long-hand. *Huh? An old-fashioned letter? Interesting.* Although I knew it wasn't polite to snoop, I couldn't help staring at the return name and address. *Mandy Crawford. 8935 Oleander Way, Mission Viejo, California 92691.*

Oh, no! My thoughts raced. I felt as if I might throw up.

Could he have a girlfriend back in the town where he'd last lived? And was the phone call from the Mandy Crawford in the letter on the table? My throat constricted as tears filled my eyes. I blinked hard, forcing them back. No, I mustn't jump to conclusions. Yet how could I help it?

I turned to gaze out the window that looked onto the side yard. In the late wintery darkness, a light from the house next door shone dimly, but I couldn't see anyone inside. An odd, lonely feeling stole over me.

I could barely make out snatches of Cam's conversation, and though I tried not to listen, I did anyway.

"So when are you coming?" I heard him ask. His voice was filled with eagerness.

I closed my eyes, wishing I could shut out the vision forming in my mind. *A girlfriend. Yes, of course!* The hurt was almost more than I could stand.

"Sorry, Jessie. I didn't mean to take so long."

I opened my eyes, whirled around, and caught my breath.

"Oh! Done already? You surprised me." My gaze locked with his. In the semidarkness, I thought I could see his face flush.

"Like I said, I didn't mean to take so long."

"No problem." I squared my shoulders, attempting a casual smile. "Where was the call from?" I blurted, then slapped my hand over my mouth.

Despite my boldness, he didn't hesitate to answer me. "Mission Viejo, California," he said, straight-faced.

Chapter Eleven

I wanted to fling something at Cam and run out the front door! Why hadn't I listened to Mike and Rocky in the first place? He really *was* using me. What a convenient acquaintance I'd been—the mayor's daughter, the perfect kid to know when you wanted to get the job done.

To make matters worse, he'd had a real girlfriend all along. She'd been waiting for him back home. In just a matter of a few short months, summer vacation would arrive and most likely she would too. Wasn't that what they'd just been talking about?

I blinked back fresh tears. "Cam, I've got to go home. It's much later than I thought." Grabbing my shoulder bag off the table, I jumped up from my chair.

"Hey, what's your hurry? We've been so busy, we haven't had a chance to talk much."

"What's there to talk about?"

"Well, for starters, my hours at New World Skates have been changed. I'll be putting in some overtime for a while. I wanted you to know that."

A brush-off! My head throbbed. I might've expected as much. That's it! He's trying to let me down easily.

I bolted towards the front door.

"At least let me walk you home." Cam's voice trailed behind me.

"Don't be silly. I just live across the street."

"But I always walk you home!"

As I dashed onto the Easton's front porch, I tried to ignore the hurt look on his face. The cold night air smarted against my flaming cheeks. Cam's footsteps thudded behind me.

"Look, Jessie, about the overtime. I need the extra money, okay?" Obviously it hadn't occurred to him I'd spotted the letter from Mandy and had connected it with the phone call. He thought the only reason I was angry was because of his job.

"We'll talk later!" I yelled back to him. I crossed the street and dashed inside our house.

In my room, lying sprawled on my bed, I cried for nearly an hour. Mom always said crying was good for you, and for once, her words made sense.

Feeling a little better, I sat up and blew my nose. I tried to sort out my thoughts. Maybe I was jumping to conclusions. Maybe things weren't as bad as it appeared. So what was there left to do? My choices were clear. I'd either drop Cam on the spot and forget we'd ever met, or I'd keep my suspicions to myself and pretend everything was okay.

The answer became suddenly clear. I loved Cam too much to risk trashing our relationship yet. I'd stick it out till I saw this Mandy, whoever-she-was, with my very own eyes!

The next few weeks, we worked every night on the proposal. Pete, Andy, Nick, and Megan agreed to recruit more skateboarders and chair the committees while Cam and I headed up the PR.

It was crazy! I'd never talked to so many business-people in my life: the city recreation director, the president of Rotary and the Lions Club, the head of the community relations department at the university—the list went on and on.

I was surprised to learn that the people were more supportive of the skate park than I'd ever dreamed. Most everyone agreed it made sense to give us a safe place to skate where we wouldn't be getting in the way. Still, as Cam had pointed out in the beginning, our one big hang-up was money. Though a few citizens had offered small donations, it wasn't nearly enough to cover the costs.

I didn't have to wait for the council meeting to know that Preston could only provide a mere fraction of what we needed. Though Dad had been quick to point that out, he'd stood by watching our efforts with what I figured must be silent admiration. Maybe it wasn't all in vain, I tried to console myself.

My biggest problem, though, was working alongside Cam, trying to act normal. My moods constantly swung from one extreme to the other. One minute I believed I was the luckiest girl alive, the next minute I felt doomed, knowing he'd undoubtedly rather be with Mandy. Every time he kissed me, I wanted to burst into tears.

If Cam noticed my moodiness, he never let on. In fact, he never again mentioned my quick exit from his house after Mandy's phone call. I longed to believe he'd put up with my behavior because he really liked me. Or did he simply not care?

At last the day of the city council meeting arrived. By then, the task force had slaved over that proposal for hours, and we were ready to give it our best shot.

"I can't stand it!" I told Megan after school as we walked home together. "Tonight's the city council meeting—I thought it'd never get here—but now I'm scared out of my wits."

We crossed the student parking lot and turned onto a sidewalk.

"Yeah, it is kind of nerve-wracking thinking about standing up in front of all those people," she said.

"Oh, I didn't mean that." I shrugged. "After making that speech to the student body last year, speaking to a few council members should be easy. Even if my dad is one of them."

"*Now* you sound confident." She giggled. "As I remember, Jessie, you were awfully nervous that day."

"Well, that was a long time ago," I reminded her. "Maybe I've changed since then. After all the stuff I've been through—helping with Dad's campaign, getting this proposal together—I'm feeling a lot more confident."

"Good." She moved a stack of pee-chees to her other hand. "So exactly why are you so nervous?"

"I'm thinking about Cam." I hunched my shoulders against the brisk March wind. Across the farmer's field that bordered our school, a multicolored kite inched skyward, soaring on a current of air.

"Cam makes you nervous?" She sent me an incredulous look. "I don't get it."

"It's not that Cam makes me nervous," I tried to explain. "I just keep wondering if this is the beginning of the end." I chewed on my lower lip. "After the city council meeting, we should have a fairly good idea whether we'll get the skate park. Either way, Cam won't need me anymore."

"Oh, Jessie, don't be silly. What makes you so sure of that?"

I told her about the letter I'd discovered in his dining room and the call from California. These past weeks, I'd nearly gone crazy holding it inside.

We turned right down Maple Street. Blowing dust whipped past us, and I squinted to keep it out of my eyes.

"Well, if he's got another girlfriend, I think you should refuse to help him," Megan said. "Let him head up the skate park proposal by himself."

"It'd serve him right, too," I said. My heart turned over. Suddenly the thought of dumping Cam made me want to burst into a new flood of tears.

"Then why not just do it?"

"I can't."

"Why not, for heaven's sake?"

I shrugged. "It's too complicated to try to explain."

She snapped her chewing gum and grinned. "Let's face it. Cam's got you hooked. Maybe Rocky and Mike were right when they said you're naïve."

"Maybe," I half-heartedly agreed, "but there's a lot more to it than that. I guess now I want to see this skate park happen as much as Cam does. Besides, what would Fr. O'Riley say if he discovered I'd backed out? He was the one who told us we needed to prove ourselves. I can't let him down."

Later that night, Cam and I took our places inside the council chambers. Biting my lip, I glanced at my watch. Seven twenty-two. Only eight more minutes to go.

The sounds of muffled conversation drifted my way. A few of the people who'd helped with Dad's campaign sat in front of us, and one of them turned around and smiled. I smiled back, feeling a funny little quiver from somewhere inside of me.

Just then Pete, Megan, and Andy wandered in and sat down at the end of our row. I had to admit, my self-confidence was slipping a little, despite what I'd said to Megan about not being scared. We simply had to make a good impression. The skaters had worked hard to get the word out. We needed lots of supporters that night to prove we meant business.

I looked over at Dad, who was positioned at the center of the table between the assistant mayor and Mr. Granley, the parks and recreation director. At the far end sat the police chief and the utilities superintendent. Everyone looked so official with their white shirts and ties and carefully typed agendas before them.

As more kids filled the empty chairs, Dad turned to Mr. Granley and whispered something in his ear.

Glancing over my shoulder, I saw that the entrance to the room was packed. Mr. Crosham, who was directing traffic inside, grinned from ear-to-ear. Pretty soon there'd be standing room only!

I nudged Cam. "Where are all those kids coming from?" I asked. "I can't believe it!"

He flashed me a satisfied smile. "Believe it. Our efforts have paid off. Don't you see what this means, Jessie? There are more kids in town who want to skate than we ever expected!"

I returned his smile, but my insides were quaking. After tonight, it'd be a no-win situation. No matter what the outcome, I'd end up losing him.

He reached for my hand, but without thinking, I jerked it back. I couldn't bear to look at him, to see the reaction that undoubtedly had registered on his face. Why, oh why, did life have to be so complicated?

In seconds the meeting was underway. The parks director talked about planting new trees on the north end of the community playground. Dad authorized an agreement for putting in a traffic light at a busy intersection, and the council proceeded to review the city's franchise agreement with the local garbage disposal.

Then it was our turn.

Cam stood up and faced the city fathers. A hush fell over the room. He began outlining the proposal. My heart twisted as I listened to him talking. He looked so self-assured standing there, his handsome face intent. He was a born leader all right. A real winner, as Fr. O'Riley had said. What I wouldn't give to know he was mine.

After location, insurance, and maintenance were discussed, he assured the council that the skaters would help with organizing fundraisers. He paused for a moment and looked down at me. "Now Jessica Williams will conclude by talking about public relations," he said. My knees shook as I rose slowly from my seat. I looked at Dad. He smiled proudly. I opened my mouth, but nothing would come out.

At last I got up my nerve. For an instant, I could almost see Fr. O'Riley sitting there next to my dad, also silently cheering me on. New courage filled me.

With quavering voice, I began. "Mayor Williams, members of the council, the city of Preston has long needed the skate park we've proposed. It will reduce the possibility of someone skating into a pedestrian or a car. It will make the shop owners happy because we won't clutter their parking lots and sidewalks." I glanced at Mr. Crosham. Nodding, he flashed me an approving smile.

I cleared my throat and went on. "Furthermore, a skate park in Preston would help remind the citizens that skateboarding is in fact a real sport. After all, it's already been widely accepted and is included in well-known competitions." I hesitated for a moment. "Finally our skate park would attract positive attention from neighboring communities that might also be considering a project like this."

Next I presented a list of the organizations we'd contacted. Though most had promised to help with the labor, they would only donate small sums of money. Would the city be willing to meet us half-way? I asked.

Scanning the room, I waited for the council's reaction. A shuffling of feet, the sound of someone coughing filled the awkward silence.

Then Dad spoke. "The most likely site for a skate park in Preston is Addleman Park because of its central location. The city can donate the 5000 square feet of land you'll need. However, a far greater problem exists. As some of you know, the number of monies budgeted for recreation is discouragingly small. Last year, we barely managed to raise enough funds through a special election to reopen the community swimming pool."

"Mayor Williams," Cam said, rising again.

"Yes?" Dad's eyebrows shot up.

"Perhaps we've forgotten another possibility. I said earlier that the skaters would help build the skate park, but that's not all we can do. We'll help raise the money. We can wash cars, mow lawns, paint houses, even hit up the skate shops to donate a few of their top name boards so we can sponsor a raffle. We can also put on skating demonstrations downtown so people can see us in action."

Cam to the rescue! His quick thinking had saved the day.

Dad's grin grew wider. A murmur of approval rippled throughout the room.

"Then the issue is not dead," Dad said heartily." I move we table the skate park project for further discussion."

"I second it," the police chief put in.

The vote was unanimous.

Chapter Twelve

"I sure hope this spaghetti feed pays off!" I said to Megan. I dumped a big pot of boiling noodles into a stainless-steel colander and added, "at least it's a nice change from washing cars."

She ripped open a big package of napkins. "You can say that again! All we've done lately is work, work, work. Just look at my nails. I can't even keep a decent coat of polish."

I couldn't help smiling. Leave it to Megan to worry about her nail polish. Still, she'd joined in our efforts whole-heartedly. She was even skating as well as I—thanks to Pete.

"Aw, poor baby," Pete teased from the corner of the kitchen. The tangy smells of spaghetti sauce filled the room. "Better not let her do dishes tonight, Jessie. Next she'll be complaining of dishpan hands."

Nick strode in from the dining room. "We've filled all the pitchers of ice water, but we're running a little low on forks and knives. Got some extras?"

"Check the second drawer down," I replied, nodding to my right. Everyone, including a few new recruits, was doing a terrific job. What I wouldn't give for Fr. O'Riley to see us now!

For the past four-and-a-half weeks, we'd worked hard on fundraisers. On Saturdays and Sundays we'd washed cars at the Shell station on Main Street, and every afternoon after school, we'd hit the pavement selling raffle tickets. Now, with the help of our parents, we were sponsoring a spaghetti feed in the basement at the Youth Services Center.

All this time, Cam was busier than ever working at New World Skates.

"I just hope all our efforts will be worth it," I said again to Megan. Secretly I feared the skate park project was dying a slow, excruciating death. "So far, we've earned just a little less than a couple of thousand dollars," I continued. "We're going to need lots more than that to meet our quota."

I'd been elected the Task Force treasurer, and I kept a close watch on our funds. Things weren't looking good, but I vowed I'd hold out till the very last moment before I let the rest of the kids know that.

"At least this dinner should bring in lots of bucks," she answered brightly. "Almost everyone likes spaghetti!" She unwrapped a loaf of French bread and began slicing it. "Is Cam going to make it in time for the raffle drawing?"

"I hope so. After all, he's the one who talked his boss into donating three skateboards for the prizes."

Because most of the people who'd turned out for the dinner had also bought raffle tickets, we'd decided to have the drawing as soon as everyone finished eating. I'd even parted with some of my hard-earned money and stuffed five tickets into the box we'd decorated with skateboard stickers. What I wouldn't give to win one of those shiny new boards!

"Cam's sure been working a lot lately," Megan said.

I groaned, then darted her a wary look. "So you've noticed too. I hardly see him anymore." My heart sank to the pit of my stomach as I continued, "I think he's trying to break me in gently. He's trying to get me used to living without him."

"Oh, Jessie, don't get all paranoid." Her voice registered impatience. "Look, I know you're crushing hard on him, but I think you need a little vacation."

"Vacation!" I nearly dropped the pot I was rinsing in the sink. "I hardly see him as it is."

"I mean a real vacation, where you can think things out. Like spring break."

I nodded. "I've been looking forward to it forever."

"Good! Then come with my family to the beach for a few days. Mom's already made reservations at one of the coolest resorts on the coast. She said I can bring along anyone I want."

I swallowed hard. Maybe a little distance from Cam would help me sort out my thoughts. "Okay. If my parents say I can go, then I'll do it! It sounds like—"

My sister popped into the kitchen, carrying three cans of ground coffee. "Can I announce the raffle winner tonight? Pl-e-e-a-se, Jessie!" She set the cans on the counter with a thud.

Grinning, I answered. "Sure. You can even draw the names out of the box." For some reason, I felt especially agreeable with my sister that night. She'd been a big help getting ready for the spaghetti feed. I don't know what had come over her—or maybe it was because I'd been trying a little harder to make her feel included.

"Here, help me with the tossed green salad," I said. "There are more tomatoes in the fridge."

She began tearing a head of Romaine into bite-size pieces.

I glanced out into the dining area, hoping Cam might show. Rows of tables with red-and-white checkered coverings and votive candles lined the room. Yet the only people mingling by the entrance were Megan's parents who'd agreed to be ticket-takers.

"Jessie, are we running short on supplies?" Mom breezed into the kitchen a minute later. "I'll run over to the store if you need anything."

"Thanks, but I think we're all set." The clock above the kitchen sink told me it was five-forty-seven. Soon the crowds would arrive. At least I hoped there'd be crowds. We certainly couldn't afford for this event to be a big flop.

For the next couple of hours, we turned out one plate of spaghetti after another. Still, Cam didn't show. If I hadn't been so busy, I probably couldn't have hidden my disappointment as well as I did.

Megan, though, wouldn't be fooled. She saw right through me, and was cool enough to let me vent.

"What a disappointment!" I said. Ceramic plates rattled as I loaded them into the dishwasher. "Cam's the one who told the city council we could take on all these fundraisers, and now he's not even here to help out!"

"He's sold tons of raffle tickets," she reminded me. "And he did turn out every time we washed cars, even though he was late."

She was right. *As usual.* He had done more than his share so far. How could I begrudge him a little overtime at work? Whisking off my apron, I peeked through the kitchen door into the dining area. Several families were seated at the tables: the man who owned the sporting goods store, the movie theater owner, the elderly couple who ran the family clothing store—and yes, even Mr. Crosham!

"Any idea how much we've made tonight?" I asked my friend. The dishwasher hummed, nearly drowning out her reply.

"Yeah, I checked with my folks a few minutes ago. It looks as if we've cleared another thousand." Her eyes held a pleading look. "That's going to help a lot—isn't it?"

I sighed. "Sure, everything helps. But we're still nowhere close to our goal. I don't know about you, but I'm about ready to quit. How much harder can we work?"

She slumped onto a wooden bench and stared down at her shoes. "Good question. We can't keep giving spaghetti dinners for the rest of our lives."

Exhausted, I sat down alongside her. Silently, I studied the brown-and-beige tile floor beneath my feet. What were we going to do?

"Hey, why the long faces? It's almost time for the drawing!"

"Cam! Where've you been?" I jumped up and threw my arms around him.

"Working." He kissed me lightly, then grinned. "I told you I might be late."

"You're always working." By then I was so overjoyed to see him, it sounded more like a statement than a complaint. Funny how quickly I could forget about my misgivings the minute he appeared.

"And now I'm ready for more," he said, his smile growing wider. "From the looks of the crowds out there, they'll be plenty of tables to wipe down and floors to sweep."

"Don't let looks fool you." I told him about the ticket sales and how far away we were from meeting our goal. I hadn't meant to color the moment with gloom and doom, but somehow it'd just slipped out.

He frowned. "Hmmm, I guess we'll have to call another meeting. See what we can do next."

I spread my hands wide. "Wait a minute! We've barely recovered from tonight." The eternal optimist. Sometimes I wanted to strangle him.

He tweaked my cheek, then took me by the hand. "Okay, okay. We'll talk about it later. Let's go into the dining room. I, for one, don't want to be stuck here in the kitchen when your sister announces the raffle winners."

Al, Pete, and Megan followed us to the back of the room. I suspected Megan had shared with them my predictions, because they were all looking glum.

"Listen up!" I announced. "Angie's ready to start."

"The first winner is . . ." Her voice squeaked as she stood before a big podium and dipped her hand into the box. "The winner is Dennis Staatz."

A kid from the front table whooped. In seconds he was sprinting up towards Angie to claim his skateboard, decorated in patterns of purple, white, and red.

The second and third winners were two of Angie's classmates from the middle school. Her face flushed as one of them kissed her on the cheek, reached for his skateboard, and sauntered back to his seat.

I swallowed hard to keep from giggling. Maybe my sister was finally on her way to getting a boyfriend!

The people began talking and putting on their coats.

"Thank goodness, it's time to go home," I murmured to Cam. "It's been a long night."

He elbowed me. "Haven't you forgotten something?"

I sucked in my breath. "Gosh, you're right!" As PR chairman, I'd planned to sign off with a quick thank-you speech. I dashed to the podium and held up my hand.

"Ladies and gentlemen! May I have your attention, please?" The din in the room fell silent. A sea of expectant faces turned to me. "On behalf of the kids who've sponsored this delicious spaghetti feed, I'd like to express my appreciation for your support." I paused, thinking back to last fall. Then, I'd never dreamed the people in Preston would do anything to support the skateboarders. "I'd also like to thank all the parents who've so generously helped us out," I continued. "Without them, this dinner wouldn't have been possible." I smiled at my parents who were seated three tables away. "Good night and thanks for coming."

"Hold on, everyone! The evening's not over!"

My mouth dropped open as Mr. Crosham sprang up from his chair and hurried to the podium. His steely gray eyes darted around the room. "I, too, want to put in my two cents' worth. These kids—the ones I used to call good-for-nothing punks—are some of the hardest working young people I've seen. Last winter when some *real* good-for-nothing punks defaced the outside of my empty store, not once but three times, these kids proved their worth by agreeing to clean up the damage. Then last month, not only did they present a dandy proposal for a skateboard park, they pitched in to raise the money."

He hesitated, wiped his brow with a handkerchief, and pulled a plain white envelope out of his pants pocket. "I would like to do my part in helping reward their efforts." He turned and handed me the envelope. "Miss Williams, please accept my donation."

* * *

"Twenty thousand dollars! I don't believe it!" I stared down at the check one more time, making sure there wasn't a mistake. The streetlight cast a dim glow in the parking lot where we'd gathered after we were done cleaning up. "Mr. Crosham's the last person on earth I thought would give us that much money."

"It's awesome, all right," Andy agreed. He crossed his arms over his chest. "Twenty grand. I always heard he had more money than he knew what do with. I also heard he hated kids and never shared a cent of his dough."

"Well, I guess you were wrong," I put in. "We all were."

"So now what?" Al asked me. "How much money do we still have to cough up?"

I scratched my head. "I'm not sure, but we're definitely getting close."

"After tonight, anything's possible!" Pete said from over my shoulder.

"For sure!" Andy said.

"I second it!" Megan exclaimed.

Cam's face was wreathed in a smile as he gave me a high-five.

We all began talking at once. It was too good to be true! Now all the planning and sweat and—yes, even the discouragement was worth it.

Hugging my arms to my chest, I exhaled slowly, then gazed up at the stars. They glittered like millions of silvery sequins.

"I'm so stoked! And this calls for a party!" Andy exclaimed. "Come over to my house. I've already asked my folks, and they said it's fine." He darted a look at some of the new skaters who'd stayed late to help us clean up. "Everyone's invited."

A bus slowed, then rumbled by. The smell of exhaust assaulted my nostrils.

"I'll bring three six-packs of Coke," Nick said. "Cam, how about picking up some chips?"

Cam slipped his arm over my shoulder. "Sorry, dudes. Count me out." He smiled, his gaze fixed on my face. "I haven't seen Jessie for days. We want to be alone."

Chapter Thirteen

Cam and I wandered away from the crowd to call Fr. O'Riley. We simply had to share our good news! It didn't matter that it was nearly ten—he'd probably still be up reading one of his favorite mystery novels like he often did when he lived in Preston.

The priest answered my call right away. "Splendid!" he exclaimed after I'd blurted out the evening's events. "So ol' Harry came through, did he? He's given sizeable donations to my discretionary fund more than once in the past. Just slipped in a little something extra, as he so often put it." He chuckled. "Is Cam there with you, Jessie?"

"Uh-huh! Wanna talk with him?"

"Right. Put the lad on."

While they chatted for the next couple of minutes, I stared at the blinking neon signs across the street. The muted sounds of traffic faded into my thoughts. It didn't make sense. Months earlier when I'd first met Cam, I'd give anything to hear him tell his friends he wanted to be alone with me. Now, though, while I should be ecstatic, a big gray cloud seemed to hover over my head.

What was the matter with me? Maybe I really *did* need that trip to the beach over spring break.

Cam ended the call and took my hand. It felt strong and warm wrapped around mine.

"I have more good news. You'll like it!"

"Oh?"

"Fr. O'Riley told me he has a month's vacation in July. He wants to drive up and help build the skate park. He says we should have the biggest part done before he has to head back home."

"You're kidding!"

"No, I'm not! Won't that be rad? We'll get to see him for a whole month again."

"Yes! I've missed him more than I ever expected to. Even if it weren't for Fr. O'Riley and Mr. Crosham and all our people who'd turned out to help, plus lots of the business owners in town—" I broke off. The list was growing. Were these people the same ones I'd been so quick to criticize in the past? Had they changed somehow? Or had I changed instead?

Later, after we'd eaten hamburgers and French fries inside Gumbo's and then cruised around for a while, Cam parked the Mercedes in my driveway.

"Wanna come in?" I asked. I gazed cautiously at the dim light shining in my sister's room. Angie had invited Priscilla to sleep-over and, though it was past midnight, I suspected they were still up talking. My sis was probably carrying on that very moment about the kid who'd kissed her cheek.

Cam's lips lifted in a half smile as he followed my gaze. "Hmm, maybe we'd be better off staying out here."

"Okay, but I'm cold." I shivered. Through the windshield, I could see a light April frost that had dusted our front lawn. Blades of grass shimmered in the full moonlight.

I snuggled closer, drinking in Cam's magnetic nearness. I felt his heart beating, heard his soft breathing. Why did he have to keep me on this crazy roller-coaster ride?

"So much as happened since we moved to Oregon," he said.

"Absolutely." I yearned to let him know how much I loved him. About all the new feelings that had blossomed inside of me. But for now, I'd have to be satisfied to keep them to myself. There was too much uncertainty looming between us.

Cam wrapped his arm around my shoulder. "And now we're really going to get our skate park," he said, staring straight ahead.

"And then what—what happens after it's done?" I couldn't resist testing him, seeing whether he'd still have time for me.

"Then everyone will live happily ever after," he replied, tweaking my cheek. "Heck, Jessie. What do you expect?"

I averted my gaze and stammered. "I . . . I just meant, what else will you be doing this summer?" This sounded ridiculous. I wasn't getting anywhere.

His arm tightened around me. Then he took my chin in his hand, tilting it up so I was forced to look straight into his eyes. "I'll be skating, working, and spending every spare minute with you. So what's on your mind?"

His mellow voice brought my defenses tumbling down. "Uh, nothing." I wanted him to kiss me and wipe away all my dark, ugly doubts. Why didn't he love me the way I loved him? The aching inside of me twisted deeper. "Nothing's wrong."

"Then why are you asking these dumb questions? After all this time, you should know me practically as well as I do."

"I . . . I just." I stopped talking and threw up my hands. "Oh, forget it! How should I know why I ask dumb questions? How should I know why I do anything? If only—"

He drew me close and silenced me with a long, slow kiss. Images of Mandy floated to the surface of my mind. I wanted to die. Is this how he kissed her too?

I eased away. "Megan's invited me to go with her family to the beach over spring break. I've decided to do it."

"Cool."

"B . . . but don't you even care? I mean, doesn't it matter that I'll be gone for almost a whole week?" My throat burned with unreleased tears.

"Jessie, I don't own you. You can do anything you want—well, almost anything—over spring break. And I *will* miss you. A lot."

I wasn't convinced. Of course, he didn't own me. And why should he? Now that the skate park was nearly a sure thing, the girl he really wanted was Mandy.

* * *

Saturday at last, the first day of spring break! As I picked my way through the mound of clothes on my bedroom floor, I plopped my empty suitcase on the bed. April on the Oregon coast could be a weather forecaster's disaster! Of course, I'd need shorts and T-shirts and my two best swim suits if the weather stayed sunny. But I should also pack at least one pair of jeans and sweatshirts and maybe even my rain jacket in case of spring storms. The only way I could decide was to yank most all my clothes out of the closet where I'd be able to get a better look.

The chiming of our grandfather clock in the hall told me it was eleven. I'd better hurry. Megan's family would be stopping by to pick me up shortly after noon.

I stacked my clothes inside the suitcase, threw in my make-up bag and curling iron. *Now what else?* Hands on hips, I surveyed my room.

Angie burst through my door without even knocking first, but I pushed my annoyance aside. "Have you seen my library book? The one about the girl who became a model?" Lately she'd been walking around the house balancing books on her head.

"Umm . . . no, I don't think so. Is it from your school library or the city library?"

"The city library. Mom wrote me a note before she left for work this morning. She said I'd better find it and give it back before I run up a big fine."

"That shouldn't be a problem for you. You've got lots of money," I teased. "It's just a lucky thing that Cam hasn't minded sharing his skateboard with me." Still, it no longer upset me that she'd kept me from buying my own new skateboard. The important thing was we were starting to get along.

Angie's eyes widened. "That's not the point. Mom's going to be home on her lunch break any minute now, and she said I'd better have that book in my hot little hands. If I don't, I'll have to take it back later myself."

The telephone rang, and I hurried downstairs to answer it. "Jessie! You won't believe this!" Megan's voice sounded as if she'd just been grounded for an entire year.

"What's wrong?"

"It's my aunt Mildred in Seattle. She's real sick, and they don't know what's wrong. The ambulance rushed her to the hospital a couple of hours ago."

"Oh, that's terrible!"

"Yeah, it *is* awful. But that's not all. Mom says we've got to go there instead of the beach. Aunt Mildred practically raised her, you know, and Mom feels responsible." She paused. "I'm sorry. I was so excited about our plans."

"Me too." Disappointment washed over me. "I understand though," I added sincerely. "I hope your aunt gets better. Real soon."

After we'd chatted a minute longer and Megan promised to call when they came back home, we said good-bye. Angie traipsed back into my room and plopped down on the bed. I shook my head, my gaze fixed on my suitcase.

"What's the matter?" my sister asked.

I told her the entire depressing story, then glanced at the mess in my room. If Mom came home before I straightened it up, Angie wouldn't be the only one in trouble. "Help me pick up these clothes, okay?" I pleaded. "Who knows? Maybe your book is buried somewhere beneath them."

A dejected look shadowed her face. "Oh, okay—but what would *my* book be doing in *your* room?"

I ignored her last question and focused on the task at hand. All-the-while, I silently reminded myself that by staying home I'd still be near Cam. Mixed emotions tumbled inside of me. Love. Fear. Jealousy. Envy. How much longer could I go on like this?

"This is stupid." Angie stomped her foot. "I'll never find my book here! I'm going to look downstairs now." She scowled, then flounced out of the room.

Heading towards my closet, a pile of clothes heaped in my arms, I glanced across the street. A yellow car with a white license plate was parked in Cam's driveway. I zeroed in on it and blinked. A *California* license plate! Outside Cam's house, a middle-aged couple stood talking with his parents.

I threw open my window. The man, who was nearly bald and wearing dark blue Levis, said something I couldn't hear. Everyone laughed. In seconds, they disappeared inside the house.

Then I caught sight of Cam sauntering out through the side door, skateboard in hand. My heart stopped. A petite blonde emerged beside him, talking animatedly. Mandy! It *had* to be Mandy! Appearing even cuter than I'd imagined her, she wore hot pink shorts and a white T-shirt with a splashy pattern that looked as if it'd been silkscreened.

So he couldn't wait till summer! I silently stormed. Mandy was here to visit now. How convenient for him, especially when he'd thought I'd be gone.

Biting my lip, I wondered whether Angie had also spotted him. A tear coursed down my flaming cheek, splashing onto my hand. Through a watery haze, I saw Cam jump onto the board and whizz down the street. Twisting in mid-air, he turned, ground the curb, and flipped onto the sidewalk.

"Perfect!" the blonde yelled.

I couldn't hear his answer, but he nodded and tucked the board under his arm again. Slowly they strode back inside the house.

I had to sit down. My head throbbed. My legs felt like Jell-O. This was it! The proof I'd been dreading.

We were definitely through.

Chapter Fourteen

"Your dinner's getting cold." Mom's voice sounded from outside my closed bedroom door. "It's your favorite, taco salad."

"I'm not hungry. Go ahead and eat without me." Buried beneath my covers, I drew my knees up to my chest and prayed she'd go away.

"But dear, what's wrong?"

"Nothing. I just want to get some sleep."

"What's the matter? Aren't you feeling well? You never go to bed at seven in the evening."

"I think it's just a touch of the flu," I answered, giving a fake cough. "But believe me, I'm fine. I just need some rest now." How could I face my family at a time like this?

"All right then. Just let me know if you need anything, okay?"

"Thanks, I will."

"Good-night, Jessie."

"'Night."

As I listened to her footsteps retreating down the hall, I squeezed my eyes shut. A fresh onslaught of tears coursed down my cheeks, splashing onto my pillow. In time, my eyes grew heavy. I felt all cried out. Seeing Cam with Mandy had really messed with my mind. The last thing I remembered before I drifted off to sleep was the evening song of the sparrows in the oak tree next to the house.

Down, down. The wind whipped by me. My wheels rattled. Then suddenly, like a bird in flight, I soared back up the half-pipe. The sky and the clouds rushed forward to meet me. I let out a whoop. I'd done it! I'd dropped in for the very first time.

The next morning I awakened with a start to the sound of my sister's voice. "Jessie, Jessie, get up!" Daylight flooded my room through the half-closed shutters. I glanced at my bedside clock. Ten-thirty!

"*I said* it's time to get up!" My sister's voice came through loud and clear from the other side of my door. "What's the matter? Are you still sick? Are you gonna sleep all day?"

"I'm awake. How could I *not* be after all your racket? And no, I'm not still sick." I rolled over and sighed. So last night's dream had *only* been a dream—a fabulous dream at that, and my sis, of course, had interrupted that too. I'd dreamed about opening day at the Preston City Skate Park, and the place had been packed. Yet I hadn't been able to find Cam anywhere. How I'd longed for him to be there for my big moment.

"May I come in?"

"Okay." I gritted my teeth.

Angie pushed open my door a crack and popped her head inside. "Cam's waiting downstairs." Her eyes sparkled with mischief. "What should I tell him? That you'll be right down?"

"Tell him to go away. Tell him not to ever come back. Tell him I've come down with the world's worst case of leprosy."

"Huh?" Her jaw dropped. "Jessie, how could you? After all the trouble I went through."

I pushed aside my tangled hair and eyed her suspiciously. "After all your trouble? What are you talking about?"

She sat down at the end of my bed. I felt the mattress shift a little. "Look, I'm no dummy," she said. "I saw Cam and that girl outside his house yesterday, just like you saw them. Last night when you wouldn't come down for dinner, I knew why." Her voice rose a pitch. "Get up! Don't keep him waiting."

I blinked. "So you really think I should give him another chance?"

"Uh-huh. I might only be ten, but I know how these things work."

"What things?"

"Let me try to explain." Her voice turned apologetic. "I feel kind of weird about the way I've messed things up for you guys. So I decided to do something about it. But Cam will tell you the rest, if you'll only give him the chance." She clasped both hands on my shoulders and pleaded, "So get up! If you don't hurry, he might take off."

Her words baffled me, but on the other hand, this was *so* Angie. Nothing held her back.

I threw off the covers and started dressing as fast as I could. "Well, I have an idea how to prevent Cam from getting bored till I go downstairs. You keep him company, okay?"

I dashed into the bathroom. Quickly I brushed my teeth, splashed cold water on my face, pinched my cheeks to bring up the color, and added a trace of lipstick. My heart was slowing inching higher and higher into my throat. What was I going to say to Cam? What did he plan to say to me?

When I saw him sitting on our living room couch, his chin in his hands, I wanted to turn and run. He looked so gorgeous, even better than that first sunny autumn day I'd caught sight of him from my bedroom window. But now my stomach was churning so hard, I wasn't sure what to do.

"Hi, Cam." The word seemed to stick in my throat.

"Hey, Jessie." He stood up, rubbing his palms against his jeans, and darted a look at Angie. "Uh . . . do you suppose we could go somewhere?"

"Never mind!" Angie interrupted in a sing-song voice. "I'm leaving for Priscilla's house. You guys won't ever have to worry about me bothering you again." She flung her shoulder strap purse over a shoulder and lifted her brow. "That's a promise, guys."

Gaping, I watched her sail out the front door.

"That's some little sister you've got," he said with a chuckle. "She was outside banging on our door shortly before nine this morning."

"Brat," I mumbled under my breath.

He grinned, then continued. "When no one answered her, she walked around by my bedroom window and shouted at me. I was sound asleep."

"Angie did *that*?" I asked, and he nodded. "Well then, that makes two of us," I added. I'd heard my parents say she was precocious, but I'd never expect her to wake Cam up too.

"Uh-huh, she gave me the old up-and-at-em routine. I think she's trying to play match-maker. She wouldn't quit hollering at me until I invited her inside."

"But what about . . ." I hesitated. "What about your company? The cute little blonde and her folks?" In my rush to get downstairs, I hadn't bothered to notice whether the car with the California license plate was still parked outside his house.

He took my hand and pulled me back down onto the couch. "She's gone. She and her parents left last night after they stayed for a quick dinner." His gaze held mine. "I guess both you and your sister thought I had another girlfriend, but I don't, I swear. That's why Angie came over this morning. To give me a piece of her mind." He squeezed my hand. "I'm sorry this is such a mess. Will you please hear me out?"

"Well, yes." If only I could believe everything would be all right.

"That girl you saw was Pee-Wee. Remember when I told you about my best buddy's girl?"

"Uh, yeah. The one who works for the skate shop back in your hometown and does graphic artwork?" My taunt shoulder muscles began to relax. "That wasn't Mandy?"

"Yes, it was. Pee-Wee and Mandy are names for the same girl."

"What are you talking about?" Confusion wrapped around me.

"Pee-Wee's real name is Mandy. Mandy Crawford. But I always call her by her nick-name instead. Just for kicks. She's barely five feet tall."

"Oh." My face warmed with embarrassment. "I remember now. You *did* explain that." Visions of Mandy's letter surfaced in my mind. "But what about the letter she sent you? Why is your best friend's girl writing to you?"

He let go of my hand. "It's nothing like you're probably thinking."

I settled back in the couch, taking in his pained expression.

"It was all my idea," he continued. "I asked her to stop by while she and her folks were passing through Portland. That's what the letter and the phone call were all about. It's spring break for the kids at her school, too, and her family had planned a skiing trip in Oregon. Pee-Wee . . . er, Mandy was simply making a special delivery."

"And I suppose besides all her other talents, she works for the United Parcel Service, too!"

"Jessie!"

"Okay, okay. Sorry. Go on."

"Before I do, there's something I want to show you. This will help explain everything." He reached down behind the couch, pulled out a long rectangular package wrapped in tissue paper, and handed it to me. "Here, open this."

"What is it?"

"Just open it.

Without further coaxing, I ripped off the paper. There before my eyes was a skateboard decorated with a gorgeous yellow-and-black butterfly in the center. Several smaller butterflies in shimmery blues and greens bordered the edges.

"Oh! It's wonderful!" I breathed. "Thank you."

"When I overheard you telling Tammy at New World Skates how much you'd like to own one, I figured if I could buy you a blank board, the kind without any designs, maybe Pee-Wee would agree to silkscreen it. It took several emails and a few snail mail letters—that's when her computer was acting up—to find just the right pattern."

I didn't know whether to laugh or to cry. "Oh! It's beautiful. Absolutely perfect! And now I understand what you meant when you said Pee-Wee made a special delivery."

"Uh-huh, it would've been expensive to send it. Since her folks were planning to drive through our area anyway, it only made sense to drop it off instead."

I felt so stupid. I wanted to throw myself into his arms and forget I'd ever mistrusted him.

"Know something?" I said. "I have a confession to make too. The whole thing that got me started . . ." I hesitated, avoiding his eyes. "The whole thing that got me started being suspicious was when Rocky and Michael said you were using me."

"Using you?" His voice was barely a whisper.

"Yes. And I was gullible enough to give into it. They said that because my dad was about to become the new mayor, you were getting on my good side—Dad's too—so you could get the skate park you wanted. But I should've known better. One of the first things you said to the skaters when you came to town was to be courteous to the older people, to show you cared about them. It only makes sense that you'd want to help with Dad's campaign too."

Cam's eyes softened as he looked down at me. "I did want to help him. But not to use you. I like you so much it wouldn't have mattered to me who your dad is. Heck, I wouldn't if you were living alone on the streets of Portland. I love you because you're you."

My heart swelled with happiness. "Oh, Cam. This is too good to be true." I suspected the reason he'd been working so much lately was to earn extra cash for my skateboard. Maybe one of these days, I'd get up the nerve to ask him. But for now, I just wanted to keep looking into his eyes.

His lips came down on mine—softly, tenderly. Eagerly I slipped my arms around his neck and kissed him back.

"Know something?" I said after we'd finished kissing. "Maybe Preston's not such a bad place after all. I mean, there's been so many people who have helped us get our skate park. People I thought in the beginning didn't understand us at all." I sighed. "Just think. There's a good chance that by the end of the summer, our dream will have come true."

"Right. I'm really stoked." He sent me a lopsided smile. "And it was all worth it, wasn't it? I knew we could do it if were willing to work hard enough. And so did Fr. O'Riley. You did too."

As I smiled again into his eyes, I nodded silent agreement. Maybe there was more in life than freedom and adventure. Like knowing how to believe in the world around you, knowing how to believe in yourself.

Maybe that was the greatest adventure of all.

The End

Don't miss out!

Visit the website below and you can sign up to receive emails whenever Sydell Lowell Voeller publishes a new book. There's no charge and no obligation.

https://books2read.com/r/B-A-KKZY-SYPWC

BOOKS 2 READ

Connecting independent readers to independent writers.

About the Author

Sydell Lowell Voeller was raised in Edmonds, Washington, and has lived in Forest Grove, Oregon for forty-plus years. Her family consists of her husband and two cats, plus her two grown sons, their wives, and four grandchildren.

Sydell has been a violinist in semi-professional orchestras, a registered nurse, and an author-writing instructor for many years. Her interest include reading, camping, astronomy, crafts, baking, and playing with her cats. Her publication history includes novels with several traditional New York publishers as well as many e-books and paperback novels.